THE JOU

The Journal

James Allen

HEADLINE
Liaison

First published in 1995
by HEADLINE BOOK PUBLISHING

A HEADLINE LIAISON paperback

10 9 8 7 6 5 4 3 2 1

ISBN 0 7472 5092 8

Typeset by
Letterpart Limited, Reigate, Surrey

Printed and bound in Great Britain by
Cox & Wyman Ltd, Reading, Berks

HEADLINE BOOK PUBLISHING
A division of Hodder Headline PLC
338 Euston Road
London NW1 3BH

The Journal

Chapter 1

It started with a cocktail party.

Gina expected it to be tedious and so began the evening with a game: dressing up. This was a game she understood and Hugo silently appreciated. She dressed in black underwear and stockings with a wicked sheen. She added a string of pearls and high-heeled shoes and for thirty minutes, before they were due to leave, she paraded around the apartment with practised unconcern.

The best part of this game was ignoring his glances and sensing his desire. She pretended to be unaware of his need to touch her and finally slipped into the black Versace dress and checked her appearance in the full length mirror.

As expected, the party was tedious but Hugo was attentive. There was never any danger of him straying for Hugo was always dependable and loyal, if a little dull, but his attentiveness this evening had an extra dimension: his lust, although he would be too polite to ever use such a word.

He touched her waist, his hand strayed over her hip. His palm slid along the upper curve of a buttock. He kissed her fingers, half in fun, and held them to his lips too long.

Gina loved him but wished he could be more demanding, more forceful. At least some of the time. He was a handsome man of thirty-five, a successful surgeon with a clinic in Harley Street, a short walk away from their apartment in North Audley Street. Perhaps if he had been in business rather than medicine he would have been more forceful, but then, perhaps she wouldn't have fallen in love with him. Perhaps being in medicine had made him more attentive than assertive.

She had fallen in love with his gentleness as well as his strong features and grey eyes. She felt the gentleness in his hands the first time they touched, a formal handshake at a party. Another tedious party. The grey streaks in his hair at his temples had made him look older than he was. He had laughed when she said distinguished.

Whatever status he had, he said, had been achieved through hard work, diligence and being a little boring. He had said it self-deprecatingly but she could tell he believed it.

Sex with Hugo had failed to live up to expectations although she had become used to its shortcomings. Like many wives, she suspected, she counted her blessings instead, but that did not stop her from playing her games in the hope of provoking a reaction.

His touch at tonight's party was insistent but unsure, as if he expected to be told to stop at any moment. In case his reaction was equally unsure, Gina took the precautionary measure of drinking too much while Hugo, as always, drank too little.

When they got home, she suggested a nightcap and poured large brandies in the final hope that the liquor might loosen his stiff shirt and libido. They took them to the bedroom and did not bother putting on the lights. She knew he was more comfortable in the shadows.

The moon provided a pale illumination and she slipped off the dress and sipped the drink. He undressed from the other side of the room but he watched intently. Gina, still pretending to be unaware of his interest, put down the glass. She unclipped the brassiere and let it drop from her arms onto the floor. The room was warm and her body felt good to be almost naked. Almost naked but not quite. It was the not quite, she had discovered, that many men found irresistible.

She bent forward to remove her shoes, aware of the swing of her large breasts, aware of the look of her husband.

'I'm tired,' she said. 'I can't be bothered with the rest.'

She'd once read that Marie Helvin had advised going to bed in stockings and a garter belt. This advice could be classed as axiom or cliché. As far as Gina was concerned, the pedantic could class it anyway they wanted: it worked.

Gina pulled back the covers and got into bed. Through half closed eyes, she watched Hugo finish the brandy and pull off the rest of his clothes. He had a good body, although he had always seemed to be unaware of the fact. He stayed trim and tanned with visits to a private health club near Marble Arch. His back was to her as he removed his undershorts. She could not see if he was aroused.

He got into bed and lay on his back. Had she played her role too well? Did he think she was asleep? His attitude to sex, even after two years of marriage, was far too deferential. She rolled against him and lay a silken knee across his thigh. Her hand stroked his smooth, hairless chest.

Gina murmured, 'What a boring party.'

'Do you think so?'

3

'Very.' She yawned and scratched her nails gently downwards to his stomach. 'I'm glad you were there. I had to go to the last one alone.'

'I'm sorry.'

'Not your fault. But I'm glad you were there. Did you see Archie looking at me?'

'No. Was he?'

'All night long. He did last time, too.' She mumbled sleepily and nestled her head against his shoulder. 'He has lustful eyes. He was undressing me all night.'

Hugo moved his arm and put it around her.

'Archie's an old friend. Very old friend.' Archie was more than fifty. 'He's been married twenty-five years.'

'He was still undressing me. Guessing what I was wearing underneath. Imagining taking off my dress. If he'd had the chance . . .'

Gina heard Hugo lick his lips and felt a tremor in his leg. She moved her knee slowly up and down as if to make herself more comfortable.

Hugo said, 'If he'd had the chance?' His throat worked silently for saliva. 'Nothing would have happened. Surely, nothing would have happened?'

'Sometimes, my darling, you are too trusting.' She kissed his ear. 'You were there so he had no chance. But if you had not been, who knows?'

Hugo tried to chuckle but it was unconvincing.

'Not Archie,' he said. 'Anyway, there would have been no opportunity. Even if I had not been there.'

'Don't be silly, Hugo. We were in a house with lots of rooms and lots of guests. It would have been easy to find an empty room. No one would have missed us.'

'But you wouldn't have gone with him. Would you?'

It was half statement and half question.

'Of course not. But he could have made an excuse to get me there. You know what I'm like after too much wine. I become silly.'

Hugo's voice became hoarse as he said, 'What could he have done? I mean, even if he got you alone in a room?'

'Who knows? With the drink and his imagination. I saw it in his eyes. Undressing me.'

She paused and sensed her husband was hoping she would continue without him having to struggle to find the words to ask her to. Gina turned her mouth to his ear and whispered, half in sleep, half in secret.

'He would have used me, Hugo. It was in his eyes. He would have pulled up my dress and touched me. He would have used me.'

Her hand casually moved lower and he shuddered as the back of it touched his quivering erection. She curled her fingers around it and kissed his neck.

'Make love to me, Hugo.'

He rolled onto his side and pushed her onto her back. He kissed her passionately and she felt the strength of his body pressing her into the mattress. His erection was against her thigh. His hand was aggressive upon her body.

'Use me, Hugo,' she whispered. 'Like Archie would have used me.'

The words released the urgency she had felt quivering beneath his skin. He made love to her but in a new and demanding way. He did not even pause to remove her panties but pulled them to one side when he eventually entered her.

His passion lasted ten frantic minutes. His caresses

became mauls. She was surprised and aroused by his intensity but, when he orgasmed, holding himself above her on raised arms so that he could look into her face, she was still a long way from her own satisfaction.

Afterwards, he rolled onto his back and regained normality in the darkness. He sighed, turned and kissed her forehead with tenderness. She remained in the crook of his arm for the requisite three or four minutes before rolling away from him and pretending to go to sleep. She could not be bothered cleaning herself. The sheets would wash.

Her intention was to wait until he had gone to sleep so she could finish what he had started, but she really had drunk too much wine and her eyes remained closed and she was claimed by dreams.

Gina awoke with Hugo on top of her once more. Her mind was confused but her body was responding. Her panties had been removed and his strokes were measured. He kissed her neck and she moaned and put her arms around him.

'Oh yes,' she said. 'Oh yes.'

Maybe this time. She moved her hips and ground her pelvis against him.

His head was buried in her neck. His hands were upon her hips.

'What would Archie have done?' he whispered in her ear.

'What?' She was still confused.

'What would Archie have done? In the room. You had too much wine. What would he have done?'

'He would have used me.'

'How?'

He pushed his penis deeper inside her as if probing for an answer.

'He would have touched me. Pulled up my dress. Touched my legs, my thighs.'

Hugo touched her legs, her thighs.

'My stockings would have sent him wild.'

He stroked her stockings and the straps of the garter belt.

'What else?' he grunted, his face hidden, his hips gaining a stronger rhythm.

'He would have thrown me on the bed and pulled off my panties.' Hugo groaned. 'His hands, his fingers, are everywhere. Inside me. On my bottom. He likes my bottom.'

Her husband's hands went beneath her and gripped her soft flesh. His rhythm increased in tempo. She was highly aroused but still not close enough.

'Then what would he do? What did he do?'

'He opened his trousers and lay on me. He put it in me. He pushed open my legs and put it in me.'

She thrust back against him, sensing he was beginning to lose control, sensing his lust overcoming his love.

'Put what in you? What did he put in you?'

The questions were hissed, as if he was demanding an obscene secret he did not wish to hear. But he did. She knew he did.

'He put his prick in me,' she whispered back. 'He pushed it inside, deep inside.' She squirmed against him. She was close now and so was Hugo. 'He fucked me.' The words were soft as a prayer. 'He fucked me.' She groaned and twisted. 'He fucked me!'

Hugo came with a strangled cry that died in the nape of her neck. He shuddered upon her for a long time and, when his limbs eventually relaxed, he remained upon her, his body enveloping hers although he took the weight on his knees and arms.

Gina's emotions reluctantly returned to normal, for she had again missed her own orgasm. For a moment she wondered why Hugo still lay upon her. Surely he did not intend doing it again?

He was embarrassed. She realised with sudden insight and from his prone body language that he was embarrassed.

'I love you,' he whispered. An atonement for his interrogation. 'I love you.'

He gave her another chaste kiss on the forehead.

'I love you too,' she replied, and smiled at him tenderly to show it was all right.

He rolled from her and to the side of the bed, his back to her as if ashamed. He left his hand trailing behind him. Gina held it and they went to sleep.

Chapter 2

Gina and Samantha giggled as they had giggled when they were schoolgirls together. Perhaps it was the red wine, thought Gina. They were on the second bottle.

They lunched once a week at the Italian restaurant in a street between Knightsbridge and Brompton Road. The restaurant was discreet and expensive enough to allow diners the space to eat and talk in comfort. Its location was handily placed between the twin temptations of the stores of Harrods and Harvey Nichols.

Usually, Sam had to return straight to the publishing company where she worked as an editor. Quite often, Gina finished the afternoon shopping. They were two beautiful women who were thirty years old, both married and still bonded by a shared adolescence.

Samantha was blonde and slim and could eat what she wanted without worrying about her figure. Gina remained on a permanent diet so that her lusher shape did not suddenly lose its elegance and droop in all the wrong places.

Which was why Sam had just eaten minestrone and garlic bread, tagliatelli, and peaches and ice cream, and Gina had had chicken and a salad.

They had been friends since Gina had been the new girl at school. Sam had befriended her with a challenge to jump in the river, that ran along the bottom of the playing fields, fully dressed. When Gina had done so, Sam had joined her. It had been, Sam said, a baptism of friendship.

'Bitch,' Gina said.

'Thank you very much. Bitch yourself.'

'You never put on weight.'

'Chance would be a fine thing.' She touched her breasts beneath the suit and Gina giggled again and glanced around the restaurant to see if anybody had noticed. 'I could do with a little more up here. Maybe I should have implants. Do you think Hugo would give me discount?'

'Your breasts are fine. You know they are. Besides, blondes have more fun.'

'Once perhaps.' Her smile was a little sad. 'Anyway, you didn't do so badly yourself for a brunette, as I recall.'

They laughed at the memories, some shared, some personal. Gina straightened the tie she wore with the two piece skirt and sweater combination. It was preppy and made her look younger.

Gina said, 'How's Brian?'

'Brian is Brian. He gets up, goes to work, makes money. Sometimes he even comes home. At the moment he's in Hong Kong. Says the potential is enormous. I remember when it was more than his potential that was enormous.'

They chuckled, and Gina said, 'How long have you been married? Four, five years?'

'Six years, believe it or not. The itch should arrive next year.' She squirmed on her seat. 'I hope he notices. Maybe

I'll buy a wig and he'll think I'm somebody new.'

Gina stopped smiling. She felt suddenly sorry for her friend. The confessions were being made in a joking manner that hid sadness.

'Is that what happens to marriage?' she said. 'Boredom?'

'Of course not. We have our careers. His in the Far East and mine here.'

At least Samantha still had a career. Gina had been in public relations but had stopped working when she married. Hugo had asked her to and she had agreed, perhaps too easily. Now, she supposed, she was a lady who lunched. It was a thought that made her wince inwardly.

Gina said, 'After all that garlic, I take it you have no heavy duty meetings this afternoon?'

'All I have this afternoon is to explain to an author that her three generation saga is two hundred pages too long.'

'You think garlic will protect you?'

'I will be telling her by telephone. She lives in Scotland. The book is good. There are just too many words.'

'Yes, there are.' Gina did not want to hear about romantic fiction. She wanted to talk about romantic fact. 'We were talking about marriage. Do all marriages end the same way?'

Sam appraised her, before replying, perhaps sensing they were heading into more serious topics.

'Not necessarily. Don't take me as an example. Good grief. I've read that some marriages work wonderfully. Or was that Mills and Boon? Of course, some divorces work wonderfully, as well.'

'Have you thought of divorce, Sam?'

'I thought about it. I decided to wait and see if things got any better.'

'Did they?'

'I'm still waiting.'

'I'm sorry.'

'Don't be.' She smiled. 'We get on fine, when he's at home. Like brother and sister. But somewhere along the line, the other part died.'

'The other part?'

'The sex. Once you stop, it's difficult to start again. Having sex on a regular basis, I mean. It becomes embarrassing.' She shrugged. 'He has a demanding job and many nights he came home tired. The nights would stretch into weeks and then he went abroad.' She smiled ruefully. 'Eventually, he suggested separate bedrooms so he wouldn't disturb me when he came home late.' She spoke as if she were quoting him: 'So I could arrange my own space without his intrusions.'

Gina said, 'Why stay with him?'

'Because I still love him. Because, in a way, he still loves me. It was good once. Perhaps it's the memories I'm in love with.'

'Perhaps it's because you haven't met anyone else?'

'I haven't looked.'

'Surely, you've been tempted?'

'Not really.'

'No affairs?'

'My memory of affairs is that they can be distinctly messy. No. No affairs.'

Gina shook her head.

'I would never have believed you could remain celibate. You of all people.'

'Well, that's not strictly true. Being celibate, I mean.' Samantha smiled and blushed. 'Imagination can be a wonderful thing.' She kissed her forefinger and pointed it at Gina. 'You meet a better class of person that way.'

Gina laughed but felt uncomfortable, even though she had wanted to lead the conversation to sex, because she had her own disclosures to make.

'Hugo and I have been married two years.'

'I know. I was there.' Sam raised an eyebrow. 'I take it your sex life is still fulfilling?'

'Oh yes. Well, I think it is.'

'You think it is? That sounds a trifle like equivocation.'

'Not really. It's just that, when we're in bed, Hugo likes me to tell him stories.' This time she blushed. 'Sexual stories.'

'Does he now?'

Samantha leaned forward, her interest aroused.

'Is that normal?' Gina asked. 'I mean, after two years of marriage, is it normal that he needs me to tell him stories?'

'Do they work?'

'Yes, they work.'

'Then I see no problem.'

'You don't think it's, well, unflattering that he needs that sort of stimulation?'

'Men are strange creatures, Gina. They can be tender and romantic but basically they enjoy crudity. They enjoy being rude. Does he like you to use rude words?'

They exchanged looks and burst out laughing.

'Yes, he does.'

'No matter how old they get, how wealthy or how powerful, men remain little boys. Being rude turns them on. Talking about it turns them on. They can't help it. That's the way they're made. We are sugar and spice and they are slugs and snails and puppy dog tails.'

She giggled and covered her mouth with her hand.

'When you think of it, whoever wrote that rhyme got it exactly right. After they've finished and all that urgency has spurted out of the puppy dog tail, what does it look like? Just like a snail.'

Gina giggled and warm memories of school days filled her and she felt closer to her friend than she had in years. And no, she decided, it was not the wine.

'So you think it is normal?'

'On a normality scale of one to ten I would rate it eleven. There are a lot worse things he could ask.'

'I suppose you're right. But it makes me uncomfortable.'

'Why?'

'Well, we started with fiction. You know, things that might have happened.' She smiled. 'We started with Archie Tindall.'

'Archie Tindall? All red hair and a pot belly?'

'Yes.' They both laughed. 'I pretended that Archie had been lusting after me at a party. I pretended he had trapped me in a room and, well, raped me.'

'Raped you?'

'Well, I said was overcome with drink and he took advantage of me.' She looked meaningful. 'I said Archie had his way with me. He used me.'

'He would be incredibly flattered.'

'Don't you dare tell him!'

'Of course not.' Samantha laughed. 'He might take it seriously.'

Gina stopped smiling.

'So might Hugo.'

'What do you mean?'

'We started with fantasy but now he wants the stories to be more real. He wants me to tell him my sexual experiences before we met. I'm not sure I want to.'

'Why not?'

'I don't know how he would react.'

'It would arouse him.'

'I've no doubt. But afterwards. What if he brooded about it afterwards? What if he changed his opinion of me? What if he stopped loving me?'

'He's devoted to you.'

'That could change.'

'Do you think it's likely?'

'I don't know. I mean, I only met Hugo three years ago. I was twenty-seven. I've had my share of lovers. If I was to disclose every sexual encounter, I don't know what he would think.'

Sam said, 'Look, I'm not prying but I had the impression that Hugo, darling man that he is, does not himself have vast sexual experience. I mean, he was a virtual virgin when you met him, wasn't he?'

'He wasn't a virgin, Sam.' Gina felt disloyal discussing her husband this way although she had asked for advice and realised her friend was trying to be helpful. 'But he wasn't exactly accomplished.'

'That's what I mean. He'd had a sheltered life until he met you.' She smiled. 'I don't mean that the way it sounds. But meeting you was probably the best thing that's ever happened to him. He marries a beautiful young woman who is sexually experienced and enjoys making love. But perhaps that's also a disadvantage?'

'What do you mean?'

'He has no real sexual experience. Perhaps you intimidate

15

him. Perhaps he wants to learn through hearing your experiences. Perhaps it would be therapeutic for him? Make him a better lover?'

Gina stared at her friend for a long moment.

'Sometimes, Sam, you talk the biggest load of claptrap I've ever heard.'

Sam grinned to show she did not take offence.

'It's that course in psychology I took.'

'You never finished it. It was a year wasted.'

'Not at all. It comes in extremely handy at the dinner table and lunches in Italian restaurants. But don't dismiss all the claptrap. I still don't see any harm in true confessions. Try innocuous ones.'

'He's not interested in innocuous ones.'

'Of course not.' Samantha corrected herself. 'He's a man. He wants rude bits.'

'Yes.'

'Then take a grain of truth and build a fantasy around it. Make the rest up. Never be quite specific. Let him wonder whether or not it is the truth.' She smiled. 'He won't ask you about them in the daylight. They'll remain bedroom secrets. Ones to whisper in the dark.'

Gina drank wine and thought about what her friend had said.

'You're probably right.'

'Of course I am.' Samantha poured more wine. 'How often does Hugo like a bedtime story?'

'About once a week. Actually, when I've had a drink and he thinks I'm tipsy. Perhaps he thinks the booze will loosen my inhibitions.'

'You have some?'

'Where Hugo is concerned, yes, I have some.'

'So the next time he asks . . .?'

'I'll tell him a story.'

Samantha prodded her wine glass across the linen cloth with a bread stick.

'I don't suppose . . .' she began, but stopped.

'You don't suppose what?'

She grinned across the table.

'That you would tell me the stories, as well?'

Gina smiled, and said, 'I thought it was just men who had dirty minds.'

'Don't be silly, Gina. And don't be churlish. Inquiring minds, if you please. And if you do feel able to tell me, will you leave in the rude bits?'

Chapter 3

The day had been hot and the evening brought no relief. The heat made them both lethargic. Hugo got home to the apartment at six thirty and showered before dinner. As he left the bathroom in a towelling robe, Gina entered it.

'Tuna and salad,' she said, as they passed. 'Al fresco. I shall wear a nightie.'

'White wine?' he said.

'Chilling.'

When she went into the kitchen he had already set the table. He had put the wooden bowl of salad that had been in the refrigerator between two plates upon which he had divided a tin of tuna. She wore a short white silk nightdress through which her breasts could be seen. He paused in pouring a white wine from Sainsbury's to stare at her body.

She smiled. A Californian wine and tinned tuna from a supermarket.

'What a high life we lead,' she said.

Hugo wore baggy towelling shorts and a T-shirt. His body was firm from the regular work-outs.

'You look good,' she said.

He laughed. 'Don't be silly.'

'No, you do. You have a good body.'

He shrugged.

'It's a body. It's functional.'

'It's rugged. It's handsome.'

'Do you want soda with the wine?'

'Yes, please.'

She brought the basket that contained French rolls.

'You look very young,' he said.

'No make-up.'

'It suits you.'

Gina smiled.

'No one would recognise me if I went out like this.'

'If you went out like that, the porter would send for the police.'

'The police?'

'To have me arrested as a paedophile.'

'Flatterer.'

'Is that flattery?'

'Now you question it, I'm not sure. Anyway, you're stretching a point. Make-up just makes me look different, not younger.'

'You could be sixteen.'

'On a very dark night.'

They ate a pleasant meal that they completed with fruit and cheese. Later, they watched a film on television. Gina continued to drink chilled white wine but left out the soda. She was aware that Hugo was watching her rather than the television screen.

Was he waiting for her to suggest they go to bed?

Would this be another night for a story?

If it was, would she tell Sam when they had lunch in two days' time?

The film lost its interest but she continued to watch it anyway, to build the tension in her husband. There was a little tension in herself as well.

Why hadn't she confessed to Sam that frequently she, too, had to provide her own satisfaction after making love with Hugo? Perhaps she would tell her on Thursday. But before then, she might have to relate something titillating from her past. What would it be?

Gina knew immediately. The memory flushed her cheeks and gave her an itch between her legs but still she waited until the film had finished before she suggested they go to bed. When they went to the bedroom, she took with her one last glass of wine.

They lay for a while, side by side on their backs in the dark, not touching. She listened to his breathing and sensed that he was nervous. Perhaps he needed encouragement?

Gina pushed the sheet that covered them down to her hips and moved restlessly. She used her feet to push the material downwards until she could kick it off the end of the bed. Hugo did not object.

'Too hot,' she murmured.

She sat up, not quite co-ordinated, and reached for a half-full glass of wine on the bedside table. She drank it and replaced the empty glass. Her hand slipped off the edge of the table.

'Whoops.' She giggled.

When she lay back on the bed, she rolled against Hugo. As usual, he was naked. He always slept naked, for comfort rather than erotic reasons. Gina nuzzled against his chest affectionately, as a puppy might. She licked his skin.

'You taste nice,' she muttered.

He quivered against her. It could have been caused by her body, her tongue or the questions he was forming in his mind. She turned round so that she lay on her side with her back towards him. She pulled his arm straight so she could use it as a pillow.

'Cuddle me,' she invited.

Hugo lay on his side and draped his other arm around her. He kept his groin away from her buttocks. Maybe he was worried that the state he was in would give away his expectations before he had found out whether they would be fulfilled.

Gina smiled to herself because she knew that would be the way his mind was working. He would feel it to be insensitive to simply push his erection against her without first discovering whether she was in the mood. Hugo had such sensitivity. And yet he only gave her orgasms by accident.

She would have thought that a medical man would have known all about sexual technique. But perhaps not. When she had complimented him upon his body earlier, he had simply said it was functional. Until now, he had treated sex the same way: an activity that was functional.

Didn't he know that sex was something more than that? Didn't he know that it was a function that worked differently for men and women?

'Are you asleep?' he said.

It was a whisper that could have been mistaken for the breeze outside. She could yawn and mumble and ignore it if she wished.

'No.'

She heard him salivate. His mouth was already dry with want.

'Tell me something,' he said.

'Something?'

What did he mean?

'From the past.' His voice was ready to crack. 'Something about you.'

'Oh. About me.'

'Yes.'

His hand stroked her arm. It massaged her shoulder. It urged her with expressive fingers.

Gina said, 'Something from the past.' Her voice became dreamy. 'Something sexy?'

'Yes.'

'About me?'

'Yes.'

His eagerness was boyish. Her power over him was pleasant. No more than that. Pleasant. The incident that was in her memory was better. Much better than pleasant. It made her tingle between her legs. Gina wanted to touch herself but knew that she could not. Perhaps she could persuade Hugo to touch her?

'It was a long time ago.'

The absurdity of the words made her stand outside herself for a second. She became an observer, staring down at the two of them lying together upon the bed in the darkened room. A grown man and woman. Hugo desperate for her to reveal the sexual secrets of her past, and she talking as if she were telling a fairy story.

But this had a better ending than a fairy story.

'I was sixteen. I went on holiday with my aunt and uncle. Aunt Brenda and Uncle Bernard. They had a villa on the Algarve. Hot days, hot nights. Like now.'

Hugo kissed the back of her neck in encouragement.

'Aunt Brenda complained a great deal. I always felt sorry for Uncle Bernard. He was a big man. I always thought him handsome but not in a sexual way. He was my uncle and so much older than me. I didn't think of him in a sexual way.'

Hugo said, 'How much older?'

'He was probably about forty, maybe forty-one or forty-two. When you're sixteen, that's ancient.'

'What happened?'

'One night, we were sitting round the pool drinking wine. Aunt Brenda said I shouldn't but Uncle Bernard said one glass wouldn't hurt. He kept topping up my glass when she wasn't looking. It was our secret. Our conspiracy.

'Aunt Brenda had a brandy. He brought it in a large glass. Lots of ice and Coca Cola and, I suppose, lots of brandy. I kept slipping into the pool to cool down. When I came back after swimming a length, she was going into the villa. She said she was tired and going to bed. Uncle Bernard told her we wouldn't be long.

'I had more wine and he said I shouldn't swim any more because it might be dangerous. I thought I was okay but when I eventually stood up, my head spun and I knew I was a little drunk. He smiled and said I would be okay in the morning, but he said that now it was time I should go to bed. I kissed him goodnight, a kiss a niece would give her uncle, a kiss on the cheek, and went to bed.

'It was hot. The window was open but the shutters closed. Moonlight came in through the slats. I took off my bikini and put on a nightdress. It was a nightdress like this. But white cotton, short. I lay on the sheet and fell asleep straight away.

'I awoke some time later. It was still dark. The night

sounds were the same. I don't suppose I had been asleep for very long. I was lying on my side. For a moment, I held my breath because I thought I was dreaming. Someone was sitting on the bed behind me. Touching me. It was Uncle Bernard.'

'Where was he touching you?'

'He was stroking my legs, pushing his hand beneath the nightdress.'

Hugo now moved closer and she felt his erection pressing against her. His hand pushed up her nightdress at the back, exposing her bottom. He lay his penis against her flesh, in the groove between the cheeks. Its heat was fierce; it pulsed. His fingers gripped her hip to hold her steady as he moved against her.

'Then what did he do?'

Gina remembered it vividly. She could smell the scent of the night, hear the insects outside the window. See the slats of light on the mattress as if she were in a prison cell at the mercy of her jailer.

But she had felt safe and excited at the same time because it was her uncle. Safe because he was a good man, excited because he was a man and she was a girl and she had enticed his touches without trying.

Years afterwards, she had visited friends who had a fifteen-year-old daughter. She had gone with the new and very temporary man in her life and the fifteen-year-old had made eyes at him. Gina had been amused and then annoyed. Later, her boyfriend had dismissed the display as innocent adolescence. He said the girl had not known what she was doing.

Gina realised she had done exactly the same with her uncle. She had used her body to flirt with him by the pool without fully being aware of what she did. Her sexuality was far more advanced than her sophistication and she had not been able to understand or control it.

Probably the whole week she had spent on the Algarve, she had innocently flirted with her uncle. But that night by the pool, relaxed with the wine, she had walked in a more blatant way, smiled and fluttered her eyelashes, and behaved as she thought a woman would behave, even though she was only sixteen.

Her uncle hadn't touched her. He hadn't slid into the water with her to engineer a collision of bodies, a playful fight where he would have an excuse to grapple with her. That hadn't been his style. She remembered him sitting on a chair in dark blue shorts and polo shirt, his skin tanned dark as the night, comfortable with his own silence after Aunt Brenda had gone to bed.

She remembered the glow of his cigar and the light of his eyes that followed her wherever she walked or sat or talked. His look was not judgmental, as grown-ups tended to be. His look was approving, admiring, loving. His look said she was an adult. That she was a young woman and not a teenager.

When she awoke in her bedroom she could smell the lingering aroma of his cigar on his breath and on his fingers as they brushed the hair from her face. His touch was so gentle, so caring. He kissed her naked shoulder. A kiss like a butterfly. Soft, imagined.

'So beautiful,' he had said to himself and the night.

She was facing away from him. Nothing sexual had so far happened, nothing untoward of which she might complain. But the situation had filled her with such desire that it had dried her mouth, as Hugo's mouth had dried, and made her moist between her legs.

Was it imagination or had all sensations been more intense back then, when they were new and undiluted by consideration, fear and indecision?

Gina had moaned and remained asleep, playing games even then, and had licked her lips with the tip of her tongue. She wished she had slept naked that night so that her uncle could see even more of her body. It was a body she felt was ripe and underused.

Boys had fumbled with her but the outcome had always been unsatisfying. She needed a lover, a man to teach her, to unleash the strange feelings that invaded her with regularity and which she eased with her fingers between her legs. She bit her lip, even though she feigned sleep. Even though she gave herself relief she preferred not to think about it, but let it happen as if by accident when the feelings got too great.

Her uncle's hand moved downwards, over her hip. It rested there awhile, upon the thin cotton of the nightdress, and she was conscious of its warmth, of its possibilities. She moaned again, restlessly, and changed her position without opening her eyes. Now she lay on her stomach, resting her face on her arms, her legs slightly spread. She had an urge to press her vagina against the mattress but resisted.

'Dear Gina,' he said. He once more stroked the hair from her face and kissed her shoulder. 'So very beautiful. Do you know how beautiful you are?'

The words were said a little louder. To challenge her to admit she was awake? She refused the challenge and steadied her breathing. She would remain asleep.

His hand moved down her back, following the curve of her spine, rising over the fullness of her buttocks. It stopped, still on the cotton, gently resting on the softness.

'Dream on,' he whispered. 'Have sweet dreams.'

The hand moved lower, over the hem of the nightdress and onto her thigh. For a moment, she thought its heat would burn her flesh. God, but it was hot. And all it was, was his hand upon her thigh.

Chapter 4

Hugo brought her back to the present.

'What did he do?'

'He pushed up the nightdress at the back, like that. He touched me there. He touched my bottom. That's it, like that. He lay upon me.' She moaned as he rolled against her flesh. 'He put it in between my legs.'

Hugo manoeuvred and his erection slid between her thighs. She tensed around it, trying to push her clitoris towards the tip.

'Then what did he do?'

'He used his fingers between my legs. At the front. There.' She directed Hugo's hand and almost cried out at the touch. 'He put them inside me.'

Her husband pushed a finger through the bush of her pubic hair and found her moist opening. He pushed a finger inside her with eagerness but little finesse.

'He did this?'

His hips moved jerkily. He seemed to have little control over them. His penis made the flesh of her inner thighs wet.

'More,' she said, without really knowing what she meant, because she was close.

He pushed another finger inside her and moved the two

29

of them in and out. Her lubrication flowed and every time he pushed the fingers in, the knuckle of his thumb brushed her clitoris.

'Like this?'

'Like this.'

He maintained the position and the movement, gasping behind her, licking her neck. She waited for the next question. Waiting spoiled her concentration.

'Then what did he do?'

Did there always have to be more?

'He put it in me.'

'He put it in you?'

'Yes.'

'He put what in you?'

'His prick. He put his prick in me.'

Hugo groaned and removed his fingers. She groaned with disappointment but he probably thought it was passion. He lifted his hips and positioned his penis between the warm lips of her vagina. He pushed it in and sank upon her with a sigh until he was totally embedded and his groin was close against her buttocks.

'Like this?'

'Yes. Like this.'

'Then what did he do?'

His voice was now urgent. His movements were on hold, waiting.

'He fucked me.'

Hugo's groan was of despair and delight.

'He did what?'

'He fucked me. My uncle fucked me.'

Hugo did the same. He fucked. He pushed her forwards onto her stomach and he fucked her. In its own way, it was exciting because she had released such forceful passion from him, but it contradicted her gentle memories and it delayed her orgasm.

Her husband rushed into his, subduing a cry as he came, dying over her shoulder. They lay together until his penis softened and began to slip from her body. He kissed her neck with the tenderness of a spent man.

'I love you, Gina.'

'I love you, too.'

He rolled from her. She slipped from the bed.

'The bathroom,' she explained.

First, she picked up the sheet from the floor and threw it over his body. He pulled it to his neck, curled on his side and didn't speak. She knew sleep would not be far away.

Gina did not put on the bathroom light. It was even darker in here. Limited moonlight entered through the venetian blind that hung at the frosted glass window. Dim slats of moonlight. She lay on the carpeted floor and her eyes closed and she drifted back fourteen years to the bedroom of a villa on the Algarve.

Uncle Bernard sat on the bed, leaned over her and placed another butterfly kiss upon her shoulder. His hand was on her thigh. It moved upwards, his fingers slipping beneath the hem of the cotton nightdress. She almost forgot to breathe as she lay with her eyes closed and lips parted.

His palm slid upwards until it caressed the curve of her bottom. It rested again, and she imagined she could feel sweat from his hand running across her flesh and making it quiver. Her abdomen twitched. Her insides were fluttering. She wondered if there were any external quiverings that her uncle could see. But it was dark. He could see little.

He raised the nightdress to her waist. She turned her

head so that he could not see her features. Even in the dark, he might feel the heat from her cheeks.

Uncle Bernard stroked the softness of her bottom. It was as if he were a blind man, determining its contours. His touch was as soft as her flesh. It did make her quiver, of that she was now certain, but she did not care. Her hips moved imperceptibly. If only he would touch her there!

His hand became a warm, snug, nocturnal animal that was exploring virgin territory. After an eternity, it moved back onto her thigh and rested once more, its fingers looped deliciously over the inside of her leg.

Gina moved on the bed.

'Stay dreaming,' Uncle Bernard warned, his voice gentle and persuasive.

She stayed dreaming but her legs parted a few inches. The snug little hand-animal moved again. It curled between her thighs and moved upwards towards the soft folds of flesh at the juncture of her legs.

Gina was close to swooning. Afterwards, she laughed because the term was so quaint but it perfectly captured her feelings at that moment. Boys had placed their hands on her thighs, even probed between her legs. In the years since the Algarve, many men had followed the same trail. But this was special. This was forbidden.

She felt sacrificial. Unable to refuse or reject anything Uncle Bernard might wish to do. He was, after all, the grown-up and she was in his care. At the same time, he had elevated her to womanhood by his looks and his touch. The situation was deliciously naughty, even dishonourable.

It helped that she remained inanimate, a sleeping object of desire. As long as she remained asleep, she could not object and he would not stop and neither of them would have to face the consequences. If she remained asleep, it would remain a dream and there would be no consequences.

His fingers slid upwards across the tender skin at the apex of her legs. They stroked the folds of flesh beneath, so gently she could have imagined it. Her bottom moved; she was not responsible, it moved in response to his touch. Her hips tilted and she raised herself slightly, so slightly he might not have noticed. She moaned and moved as if in sleep to cover the reaction, to lay her weight on her left hip and slide her right knee up the bed.

Often she slept this way. Would he believe that? Would he believe she was still unconscious? He did, he believed. For the hand continued to move.

'Sleep, Gina. Sleep,' he murmured. 'Have sweet dreams.'

A finger was in the undergrowth of her pubic hair. Its movements were unhurried. A second finger joined the first. They moved as if they sought a path without wishing to disturb her, but she was disturbed. She had to remind herself to keep breathing.

At sixteen, she always seemed to be moist between her legs. His finger left the undergrowth and found the ridges of her lips. It ran along the valley between them and they parted and again she almost swooned. She was so moist she felt she might flood the bed.

Her uncle was doing this, was touching her while he thought she slept. She wanted to push herself back upon the finger but knew she could not. This was forbidden. He should not be touching her this way and because it was forbidden it was the most exciting moment of her life. But it had to remain secret, she knew that. No one must be aware of what was happening, of what was to happen, not even her.

His finger delved between the lips into the heat and damp. It moved lazily, swimming for a moment, before following the channel deep between her legs towards her clitoris, that beautiful little beast she had discovered only the previous year.

Did Uncle Bernard know it was there? None of the boys she had allowed to touch her knew the existence of her greedy little beast that liked to be touched and rolled and rubbed until it sent her into ecstacy. But he did. He knew.

Did every girl have a little beast between her legs? Did every woman have one? Did they wear out? Or did they lose their efficacy with overuse? Was that why Aunt Brenda was so bad-tempered?

Oh God, but she hoped hers never wore out. It was her best friend and most reliable lover. And Uncle Bernard's finger was moving towards it.

He reached it and smeared it with the juices that his finger carried. She shuddered and pretended it was a dream. He rolled it, ever so slowly, with the tenderness of knowledge. She bit her lip and turned her face into the pillow. He let her sway on the brink for long seconds with his fingertip caress and she felt contractions in her vagina and wanted to cry out, to beg him, to push herself against his hand.

But she sensed the purpose of the delay and remained prone, remained a sacrifice, and felt the tension grow, the electricity course through her body until every part of her felt as sensitive as the little beast between her legs. When she felt she could endure no more of this exquisite torture, he rolled the bud and pressed it and she bit the pillow and came.

This time she could not hide the shudders that racked her but Uncle Bernard did not seem to notice. The hand remained burrowed between her thighs while the other stroked her hair and he whispered 'sweet dreams' like a mantra.

At some point during the coming Gina felt she really must have swooned for when her senses returned she was alone. She drifted on that delicious afterflow of orgasm and lay wondering if he was still in the room. Her senses said he had gone and eventually she pretended to stir from sleep and rolled onto her back and saw the room was empty.

The door was closed and her nightdress was no longer around her waist but lay decorously around her thighs. Her nostrils flared for a hint of the aroma of his cigar but could not find a trace.

Had she imagined it? Had she really dreamed that her uncle had touched her to orgasm? Her hand went between her legs and confirmed her dampness. Her fingers found her little beast and confirmed her arousal. She moaned. It still wanted to play.

Gina touched herself gently as her uncle had touched her in the dream and she knew it had been real. The slats of light still fell across the bed and across her body and she was still a prisoner at the mercy of her jailer and her fingers became more demanding and more intimate and this time she would not delay for there was no need.

She came and her senses soared and as they threatened to return to earth her fingers played the beast and she came again and again with the memory of her uncle's hand upon her body.

The coolness of the bathroom made Gina aware that she still lay upon the floor. The three swift climaxes she had wrought had left her with sweat upon her body that was making her shiver, even though the night was hot.

For a while she remained on the floor, staring at the darkness of the ceiling. Should she settle for this? Stealing satisfaction on the bathroom carpet? She had known accomplished lovers in the past, but sadly, she had not loved them. She sighed. Hugo had faults of which he was unaware and he was less than accomplished as a lover, but he was the one she loved, whether she liked it or not.

Falling in love with him had not been a decision she had made. It had just happened. Perhaps she had known too many men and God had decided it was time for her to settle down. But she could not complain. In every respect but one, she was happy with her husband.

Did that mean she had to settle for the bathroom floor?

Why was sex so difficult to talk about on a one-to-one basis? Why was it so difficult to say, excuse me darling, but you're not doing that right. And really, that leaves me cold. How about doing this? How about putting that there?

It was difficult because the sexual ego was so fragile. Approached from the wrong direction and with a lack of sensitivity, it could be damaged for life.

Gina had thought that Hugo's reluctant passion before marriage was because he was a gentleman of the old school. She had since discovered his lack of enthusiasm was because he wasn't very good at it. She was so experienced that she had been loath to be a teacher for fear he might ask where she had graduated.

How any man could pass thirty without having had an active and varied sex life she did not know, but Hugo had.

Perhaps that was why he was so successful. He had concentrated on his career and built a considerable reputation at the expense of amorous conquests.

But she loved him.

Gina got up and used the lavatory and the bidet and went back into the bedroom.

He was asleep and snoring gently. Her heart filled simply by watching him sleep. For all his faults, he was her man. But she wished the future might hold more for her than counting her blessings, although they were many. She had wealth, position and an enviable lifestyle, except when it moved into the boudoir.

The stories she told Hugo had excited him into displaying more passion than normal and had already developed his appetite for sex.

Perhaps they could also be the basis of an education?

Chapter 5

Gina went to the health club near Marble Arch the next morning and left Hugo in his study. The possibilities of education which she had nurtured the previous night no longer seemed so viable in the warm light of day.

The stories seemed a natural extension of her life which, she was beginning to believe, had become a series of charades.

They had shared coffee at breakfast and she had declined a croissant; he had read *The Times* and she had read the *Mail*, and nothing had been said about the secrets of the night before. As on the Algarve with Uncle Bernard, there had been no acknowledgement.

She kissed him goodbye and began another day of useless indulgence. Before she met Hugo, she had at least had the opportunity to be creative. Samantha might scoff, but public relations had been challenging and rewarding and she had been good at it.

Maybe she should make some phone calls. Her reputation was still valid. Maybe she could undertake freelance work.

Hugo had gone to his practice when she returned at lunchtime. The door to the study was open and a coffee cup was on his desk. She picked up the cup and hesitated when she saw the maroon leather-bound ledger that lay next to it. She did not recognise the ledger and it looked out of place. A fountain pen lay upon it.

Gina moved the pen and opened the book. It was no ledger and no diary. The pages were lined. Hugo had dated his first entry. It had been made three weeks ago. She felt as if she were prying but was too curious to turn away. Besides, if it had been private, he wouldn't have left it out for her to see, would he? Unless by mistake.

She put the cup back down and sat in the chair at the desk and read the first entry:

This journal will be a record of sexual and emotional advancement. At least, I hope that will be the case. As it is a private journal, it will also be a confessional and I have much to confess. But not yet, not until I have tested my own convictions. When I am ready I will confess but I am not ready yet.

An explanation would seem in order as to why I should be prompted at this time of my life to begin such a journal. It has come about because of a combination of events and perceptions. The catalyst was my wife's behaviour two nights ago.

We had been to a rather dull party. In truth, I would have preferred to have remained at home and ripped off the dress she wore, for what she wore beneath it had me trembling all through the evening. And yet when the opportunity arose to reap the fruits, so to speak, when we were lying in bed, I became frozen, as I do all too often. I could neither articulate my desires or comprehend Gina's mood.

There. A small confession.

But on this occasion, it was Gina who provided the prompt. She had drunk perhaps a trifle too much alcohol and was, perhaps, not aware of how disturbing were the words she said, but she began to describe the lusts of a mutual friend. She described how this friend persistently stared at her, as if undressing her, as if he was imagining what she wore beneath her dress.

This was disturbing and exciting. I doubt if I would have taken it further except that Gina seemed talkative and receptive because of the wine. I still do not know how I managed it, but I persuaded her to go further in imagination. To describe what would have happened if our mutual friend had had his way. She did describe it. Vividly.

We made love. A silly saying, but we made passionate love. The words were an incitement, they made me jealous and possessive. I possessed her. The words were a stimulant. They still are!

I open this journal in the hope that she can be persuaded to tell me more stories. Some, undoubtedly from imagination, but, I hope, others from personal experience. The thought of other men making love to my wife is the headiest aphrodisiac that I have encountered.

Yet I do not believe it to be at odds with my love for her, for the episodes I hope she will recount are from the past and the past is another country. These were not infidelities but experiences I wish fervently to share.

From now on, I will write my own account of the stories she tells me. This will be a journal of love and desire.

Gina turned the page and found that Hugo had written his

version of the fantasy of her being seduced by Archie at the cocktail party. She was shocked and aroused at the same time.

Hugo had expanded the bare facts she had provided and added details of her underwear and descriptions of her body. He had brutalised the imagined coupling between her and Archie. But he had remembered her dialogue exactly and had used it in full. Hugo liked to use the work 'fuck'.

The next entry followed the second story session and the third recounted the fantasized version of being touched by Uncle Bernard.

Hugo's account was full and, again, he had remembered and used the words he seemed to find most crucial: 'He fucked me!'

His literary style was quite good, if a little formal, and he had again fleshed out rather well the bare bones of the story outline she had provided.

At the end, he had made his latest entry. It started and ended with exclamation marks:

!This is the best so far. The most exciting, the most liberating, for I believe this to be the truth. God, how the story tormented and aroused me.

I hope for more stories, more true stories from the past. I hope Gina can be persuaded to talk further and with great detail about the men she has known and what they did.

But Uncle Bernard! I have relived that night again as I wrote it down and have become aroused again. I will have to take another shower to calm myself. It would be marvellous to be able to re-enact that episode from Gina's teenage years.

It would be marvellous to discover a collection of home videos of all her indiscretions. Photographs of her in bed with other men. But that is pure fantasy.

A re-enactment is not.

Perhaps one evening when I am delayed from coming home, I could telephone to say I will be late. Probably not back until ten o'clock. And Gina would say she would have an early night. (I am becoming aroused again, thinking about it.) When I get home, she will be lying on the bed in a white cotton nightdress and I will silently do what Uncle Bernard did. Gina will remain asleep throughout, never stirring as I touch her. As I fuck her!

What a beautiful fantasy. A fantasy that might (dare I hope?) one night come true!

The journal was a revelation. She closed it and put it in the desk drawer with a feeling of guilt at reading her husband's secrets. He said he had become aroused again and would have to take another shower. Perhaps that was why he had forgotten to put it away?

Gina took the coffee cup to the kitchen and switched on the electric kettle. She put a tea bag in a mug and listened to the steam begin to rise. A nice cup of tea was what she needed. But she knew she was pretending to herself by going through the mechanics of making a drink. She went back to the study and sat behind the desk. She took out the journal and read it again from start to finish.

Knowing her husband had written it and knowing that writing it had aroused him, also aroused her. She noticed that the quality of his writing had changed at the moments where he had been most excited. Had he really taken a shower? Or had he masturbated? Her fingers went between her legs and she touched herself through her dress.

No. She couldn't. Not in the middle of the day. She simply couldn't.

She left the study and made the cup of tea but it didn't help. What she had discovered deserved more than a cup of tea. She poured herself a large gin and tonic.

Her husband had amazed her. Perhaps this was a turning point in their marriage? In the journal he hinted that he realised there was a gap between his knowledge and her experience. But to actually begin writing a journal devoted to, how did he put it? – sexual and emotional advancement – was a great step forward.

Gina shuddered and imagined Hugo in the shower while she was at the health club. Her fingers began to steal back across her lap when the telephone rang. It was her husband.

'I'm sorry, darling, but I'm going to be late home. Something's cropped up.'

'Oh?'

For a moment, Gina was at a loss.

'You hadn't made any plans for tonight, had you?'

'No. Of course not.' He knew she had no plans for tonight. 'What time will you be home?'

'It could be as late as ten. Don't keep dinner. I'll grab a sandwich. I'm sorry, darling.'

'That's all right, Hugo.' Composure returned. 'I'll have an early night. I've been tired all week.'

'You're not ill?'

'No, it's probably the weather. The heat gets me down. If you don't mind, I'll take a sleeping pill and go to bed before you get home.'

'Not at all. If that's what you want to do.' There was a

pause. 'I'll try not to wake you.'

Gina laughed gently.

'You won't wake me, Hugo. You know me, when I've had a pill. I could sleep through doomsday.'

They shared a brief silence.

'See you later,' he said.

'Yes, see you later.'

'I love you, Gina.'

'That's nice to hear in the middle of the afternoon. I love you, too, Hugo.'

When she put the telephone down she didn't know if she would be able to last until ten o'clock in the evening. She drank the gin and poured another.

Was his call intended to prepare the way to make his fantasy come true? Had he left the journal out on purpose for her to find and read? Was this part of a plan? Or had something really cropped up to make him late home tonight? Was this simply a coincidence?

Gina couldn't wait until tonight to find out. She went into the bedroom and pulled the curtains closed to throw the room into shade. It was cooler in the shade, she told herself, as she undressed. Her face was red and she dare not look at herself in the mirror but she couldn't wait until tonight.

When she was naked, Gina lay on the bed and closed her eyes. Had Hugo only had a shower that morning or had he released his tensions in a different way? Her fingers went over her stomach and into the pubic jungle.

After all these years, it still did not take much to make her moist. Her little beast was waiting.

Chapter 6

At ten o'clock, Gina lay on the bed. She had kicked the top sheet down by her feet and lay half on her side and half on her stomach. Her back was to the door.

She wore a simple white cotton nightdress that she had bought that afternoon from their corner shop. It was a standing joke between them to refer to Selfridge's in Oxford Street as their corner shop.

The nightdress reached her thighs. She had removed all her make-up and had tied her shoulder-length hair back in a ponytail. In the dark, she could be sixteen again.

Had she got it wrong? Or was this what Hugo wanted?

In her imagination, she transposed her husband for Uncle Bernard and remembered the caresses that had taken her to the most vivid orgasm she had ever experienced until that time. Of course, the scene in which she was now waiting to co-star would not be like that, for she had told Hugo only part of the gentle truth and had enlarged it into the detailed story he had wished to hear.

She was languid after her afternoon indulgence but still filled with desire. Doubts crossed her mind like shooting stars. Had she got it wrong? Surely not. This was what Hugo wanted.

A key turned in the lock of the front door. She had left intermediary doors open so she would be able to hear. Another doubt suddenly invaded. What if this was not her husband? What if this was a burglar, an intruder?

What would an intruder think if he moved stealthily through the apartment until he came to the bedroom and saw her laying there half naked? He would be unable to resist. He would rape her.

Would she still pretend to be asleep? It would be the best option in the circumstances. She would remain stubbornly unconscious and keep her eyes closed and allow him to do whatever he wanted to do to her.

The thought made her shudder with a strange mixture of desire and fear. Someone was moving through the rooms. Was it Hugo? Or a stranger?

Whoever it was, they were at the bedroom door. She could sense their presence. She heard an intake of breath. The floor creaked as he came closer. Now there were other sounds. He was removing his clothes.

Gina kept her eyes closed and regulated her breathing. She felt vulnerable and desirable. She felt sexual. The tingles were back in her stomach and she knew she was already moist between her legs. Because she had endowed this whole scenario with so many doubts she was still not certain that the man removing his clothes at the side of the bed was her husband. She shuddered at the obscene possibilities if it was not. If it was really a stranger.

The mattress sank as the man sat upon it. A hand stroked her shoulder and arranged the ponytail down the middle of her back. The man was breathing heavily, although attempting to control noises in his throat. His desire was so strong that whimpers kept escaping.

He slid his hand down her back, over the curves of her body. Into the small of her back, and over the rise of her hip and onto her thigh. The hand crossed from cotton to flesh. He sighed and the hand stayed on the flesh.

And still Gina did not know.

Her insides were melting. She did not want to know. This could be Uncle Bernard, it could be a rapist, it could be her husband. Indeed, both Uncle Bernard and her husband could be accused of being rapists for the manner in which they had used and were using her unconscious body.

To be used. Either willingly or without choice. To lay there and accept whatever was to happen. Except, please God, let orgasm happen.

The hand slid beneath the nightdress and caressed the softness of her bottom. Another whimper escaped the man's throat. The mattress moved as he shifted and she could feel his breath upon her thighs. He raised the nightdress with the back of his hand and she realised he was looking beneath it.

He was stealing looks her husband could take any time. He was being sly and devious and exploiting her in her sleep. She tried to hide a shudder beneath a stifled yawn. The hand stopped. The man froze. He waited, his fingers spread upon her softness. When she remained asleep, the fingers dug gently into the flesh.

Now he used both hands and lifted the nightdress to her waist, laying her posterior bare. Both hands stroked the softness. He bent his head again and kissed the flesh. Soft kisses that became wetter. Open-mouthed kisses. He licked her buttocks and lay his face against them.

A hand went between her thighs and she groaned in slumber and parted her legs. Fingers reached up towards her vagina and its lips opened almost before they were touched.

Gina wanted to moan as the fingers slid into her dampness from behind as Uncle Bernard's fingers had pushed inside her all those years ago. Two fingers moved within her, encouraging her wetness. Her hips moved of their own accord. She wanted the probing fingers to discover her clitoris but they were removed too soon.

The man spread his body on the bed and lay alongside her. She felt his hip against the softness of her buttock and then he moved, almost precipitously, and lay himself against her back. His erection was huge and fierce. It burned in the groove between her buttocks.

His hand went over her hip and into the valley below her stomach. The fingers went to her vagina again and, this time, they brushed past the little beast of her clitoris, causing her to contract and move her bottom and moan again from deep within her dreams.

Two fingers pushed inside her and she adjusted her position to accommodate them. The fingers moved roughly, demandingly and she bit into the pillow. The man nudged her legs further apart with his knee and his penis slipped between her thighs. He sank upon her and he sighed into her ear, his breath hot and smelling of whisky.

The thought that she still did not know the identity of her seducer made her stomach contract. It might be her husband but it might also be a stranger. Whoever it was, she would remain silent and subservient. She would remain a sexual object, without identity. A woman upon whose body this stranger could work out his fantasy. And, while he did, Gina would concentrate upon her own fantasies: of seduction, of coming of age, of gentle coercion.

He fumbled between her legs and held the shaft of his penis in his hand to feed its head between the lips of her vagina. It went in easily, her wetness encouraging its intrusion. This time, he was unable to stifle the trembling whimper that escaped from his throat.

For a long moment, he did not move, but remained embedded deep inside her, the hardness of his abdomen resting against the softness of her buttocks. His hand held her hip, as if to steady himself, and then he began a steady rhythm, a rhythm of control. He was going to make it last, despite the trembles she could feel in his body. Gina kept her eyes closed but her lips parted and she moaned in her sleep and moved her hips in inducement, a reaction to a dream. Still she did not know, did not wish to know, the identity of her dream lover who now kissed her neck with whisky breath and whose hand moved beneath her to palm a breast through the cotton of the nightdress.

He pulled at the cotton shift, raised it so that his hands could roam beneath and find the nakedness of her bosom. His thumb rubbed her nipple into erection, his hand gripped the globe of flesh.

She moaned and twisted a little beneath his strength and he increased the rhythm, grunting with a deeper animal passion now that the tenderness was passing.

Perhaps he thought he had really penetrated her sleep as well as her body; perhaps he thought he should get it over with before she awoke? His strokes became harder. His hardness slapped against her softness.

Gina twisted, but gently, still within a disturbed sleep-state, and just enough to press her clitoris upon the bed and provide the extra pressure for which the little beast had been waiting.

This time she was taking no chances. Gina had primed herself all day until she felt she could manufacture an orgasm with a thought rather than a touch. The delicious depravity of maybe being taken by a complete stranger and the bizarre drama of the silent situation, filled the room with an atmosphere of high eroticism.

That was the stimulation that had allowed her to wait on the upper slopes of ecstacy. She pushed her little beast against the bed, her lust touched its peak and she rolled over into the furnace of orgasm. Her open mouth released her moan into the pillow and her vaginal contractions took her lover-rapist by surprise.

He gasped, his rhythm faltered and he attempted to hold himself in check but he was lost. He relinquished his grip upon her breast and he held her hips and heaved with desperate passion. She felt his penis stutter within her and he groaned and spooned around her back and shuddered into a long ejaculation.

He quivered upon her like a drowning fish that has been thrown onto the bank, without control of his limbs or his thoughts. Slowly, he subsided. His breathing normalised, the grip of his hands relaxed.

Gina had to remain asleep. She had to stay in character, no matter who had just taken advantage of her. Her eyes remained closed and her breathing sank to a satisfied lisp. She had to remain immobile until the man behind her resolved the situation, one way or another.

He withdrew from her and moved off the bed. He covered her with the sheet and left the bedroom, closing the door behind him. She lay in the darkness and strained her ears to find out where he had gone and what he was doing.

His departure had been silent and swift. She rolled over

and looked at the floor beside the bed but he had taken his clothes with him. But where was he now?

Gina remained in bed, her inner thighs slick with sperm. Her fingers lazily spread it, swam in it, dipped inside herself to find more. Her fingers found that her little beast was still awake.

They rolled it and lubricated it and once more imagination and the reality of her fingers combined to take her into another orgasm, softer and less urgent than before.

She had to remain in bed and remain in character. A sleeping beauty, ravished by a prince. She remained so much in character that, after the long anticipation and the orgasms, she fell asleep.

Chapter 7

Mario the head waiter was attentive as always. Gina wondered if he had fantasies, as well. She supposed most men did, but the fantasies of her husband still surprised her. The waiter felt her looking in his direction. He stared across the room and smiled in anticipation.

Did she want anything?

No. Nothing, thank you. Well, perhaps a peak into your mind?

He was small and squarely built. Thick dark hair and complexion and a handsome face. He was always respectful towards them but his eyes were so bland she knew he shrouded his desire.

Who figured most prominently in his fantasy, she wondered? Herself or Sam? She subconsciously straightened in her seat and pushed her breasts forward before she realised she was competing in her own mind games. This was getting silly.

It was another two-bottle lunch. Gina had insisted.

Sam had been persuaded.

'Well, all right,' she said. 'The stuff I'm doing this afternoon is probably best approached through a haze.'

'What are you doing?'

'Suggested re-writes to a family costume saga with elements of Gothic horror.'

'Sounds unusual.'

'How diplomatic.'

They had finished eating and were at the coffee and serious gossip stage.

'I have something you may want to publish.'

'What? Don't tell me you've started writing? The house-wife in the kitchen writing romance between washing-up and baking bread?'

'Bitch.'

'Sorry. I just can't imagine you writing.'

'I haven't. Hugo has.'

Sam waited for a punchline but Gina made her wait.

'Hugo has started writing?'

'Yes.'

'Last week, you told me Hugo had started asking rude questions.'

'He still does.'

'The rude questions and the writing wouldn't be linked, would they?'

'You're too clever by half.'

'I'm in a business where it pays to have an intuitive mind.'

Gina picked up the leather Hermes satchel she carried instead of a handbag, opened it and took out sheets of paper. She handed them to Sam.

'I photocopied them this morning.'

'How convenient.'

Sam lapsed into silence and began to read. Gina sipped her wine and chewed her lip. She found herself looking at Mario again. Again he smiled and raised an eyebrow but she shook her head. Unless she controlled herself, he would think she was attracted to him.

Was she? Could she be? How would he rate as a character in one of Hugo's bedtime stories?

Her husband had left early and she had gone into the study and found the journal in the drawer of the desk. She had copied what he had written on the machine in the study.

Even while she was copying the pages, she had not known if she would actually show them to Sam. It seemed disloyal to her husband. The journal was private, although she guessed he had left it for her to discover. But should she be showing its contents to her friend?

Sam finished reading.

'Wow,' she said.

Her cheeks had a blush that had nothing to do with the wine.

Gina said, 'I'm already sorry I showed it to you.'

'It's safe, Gina. I won't tell anyone.'

Her friend was serious.

'It's just that, well, it's one stage further on.' She shrugged. 'I suppose I need to talk about it.'

'That's understandable. Where did you find this?'

'He left the journal on his desk in the study.'

'For you to find?'

'I think so.'

'Well, at least you know what he wants. What he's trying to achieve.'

'What?'

'A discreet dialogue. He obviously finds talking about sex too embarrassing. Writing about it is easier for him.' She looked at the pages she still held. 'In a way, it's an on-going love letter.'

'But he wants me to tell him what I have done with other men.'

'So? It turns him on. That sort of stuff turns on a lot of men.' She coughed. 'I must admit, reading about it has turned me on.'

'Sam!'

The two young women stared at each other and began giggling. Sam topped up their glasses with wine and glanced back at the pages.

'He says this is a record of sexual advancement. It implies he knows he has much to learn.'

'Not necessarily.'

'Well, it's open to interpretation, but that's my interpretation. Maybe he's trying to improve his technique because he knows he's a lousy lover.'

Gina gave her a warning look.

Sam said, 'Sorry. Out of order. Wrong assumption. Strike that from the records, m'lud.'

'Actually, he's not very good.'

'Then it makes sense. And he's honest about it. He says the stories are disturbing and exciting. They made him jealous and possessive. They made him love you more.'

'They made him want me more.'

'We're back to interpretation again. But look at this line: "A journal of love and desire." My God, Gina, a lot of women would be delighted if their husband wrote something like this about them.'

Gina sipped the wine.

'The last entry,' she said. 'About a beautiful fantasy he wishes would come true.'

Sam looked at the pages again.

'Yes?'

'It came true last night.'

'You played it out?'

'Yes.'

'Just the way he suggested?'

'Yes. He called and said he'd be late. I said I was tired. That I'd take a sleeping pill and have an early night.'

'And?'

'And someone came in at the appropriate time and I pretended to be asleep while they had their wicked way.'

'Someone came in? Don't you mean Hugo came in?'

Gina smiled.

'I don't know. I was asleep, remember? My eyes were closed and he had me from behind.'

She blushed and bit her lip as the intimate detail slipped out.

Sam smiled knowingly.

'You enjoyed it, didn't you? You played your own game. A not-knowing game. Didn't you?'

'Yes, I enjoyed it. But it's still a strange way to behave.'

'Good God, Gina, it works! Don't knock it. It's something you both got off on. Right? I wish Brian had half the imagination.'

'Do you? Really?'

'Yes, I do.'

'If the roles were reversed, would you tell stories? Pieces from the past?'

'Yes, I would.'

Sam was serious again.

'And you would go along with this . . . this discreet dialogue?'

'This is called communication, Gina. Many couples don't talk. At least you are sharing words, ideas, desires. Hugo is exploring new frontiers. Help him and enjoy it at the same time. If it stops being enjoyable, then stop telling him stories.'

Sam was right. Gina had made up her own mind but had wanted her friend to say she was right, had wanted her own conclusions confirmed.

Sex was a difficult subject to discuss between man and wife, even between close friends. She wondered if men were equally reticent among themselves, or if they confined themselves to the crude generalities she had sometimes overheard in bars.

Perhaps this was an appropriate time to delve into the subject further with Sam.

'Can I ask you something personal?' Gina said.

Sam's look was guarded.

'We're being serious now?' Sam said.

'Yes.'

'Okay. Ask away.'

'You have had quite a few lovers, haven't you?'

'Well, I wouldn't say an exorbitant number, but I had my share before I got married.'

'The sex. Was it always good?'

'Good? That's a relative term. Sometimes it was better than others, sometimes frankly disappointing. It depends what you mean by good.'

Gina smiled apologetically.

'I'm not putting this particularly well, am I?'

'I don't know. Whatever you want to know, Gina, just ask me.'

'Okay.' She took a deep breath. 'It's about orgasms. Did your lovers always give you an orgasm?'

'Ah!' A light dawned in Sam's eyes. 'It's that sixty-four-thousand-dollar question. The one that women's magazines always ask a cross-section of readers at least once a year: 'Are you getting yours?' I wonder where they find the women to ask. I mean, who qualifies as a cross-section?'

'What's the answer, Sam?'

'Actually, I don't know. John Donne may have said no man is an island but I think every woman is. We're all different. An endless archipelago of islands, each one different. The trouble is that the male explorer who discovers the first thinks all the rest are the same. We're not.'

'You're not helping, Sam.'

'It's the wine. It makes me literary.'

'It's your job that makes you literary.'

'Gothic horror and ripped bodices? I'll have another glass.' She drank more wine. 'I'm sorry. We were being serious.'

'Trying to be.'

'All right. Well, I think the research has probably got it about right. There are some lucky ladies who can come with great ease at the mere insertion of a stiff prick but most of us, and note I include myself, cannot. Most of us need external stimulation. That's why the clitoris was invented. That's why the African Kikuyu believe in female circumcision. Cut out the clitoris and get a faithful wife.'

'They don't, do they?'

'A confirmed tribal practice.'

'My God, how barbaric.'

Gina quivered at the thought of losing her own.

Sam said, 'You could look upon the practice as a tribute to the power of the pleasure bud. Another, more gentle tribute, came from William Randolph Hearst. He was so infatuated with film star Marion Davies that he called her clitoris Rosebud. A delicate secret between lovers until Orson Welles found out and used it in *Citizen Kane*.'

'You know a great deal about the subject.'

'I once turned down a book called Rosebud. But I'm still a fan of its function. I even tried French ticklers. BB of course.'

'Pardon?'

'Before Brian. I tried the whole gamut of condoms with a particularly adventurous poet. French ticklers and all their derivatives. They don't work.'

'I'm sorry, Sam, but what's a French tickler?'

Sam giggled.

'You know, condoms with extra bits on that are supposed to rub you in the right place and send a lady wild. They do not bloody work. The things that work best are a tongue or a finger, take it from me.'

Gina grinned at Sam's exposition and the way the conversation had drifted.

'You make me feel like a beginner.' She glanced across the restaurant. 'I wonder what Mario would think if he could hear all this.'

Sam laughed and glanced towards the pay desk where Mario waited to be summoned, before looking back at Gina.

'I wonder what Hugo would think,' Sam said.

Gina knew the observation was much more to the point.

She said, 'I suppose I'm like you. Unless the circumstances are exceptional, I need external stimulation.' She smiled to herself. They had gone so far, it seemed silly not to go that little bit further. 'In fact, I also have a name for my clitoris.'

'What?' Sam was captivated. 'You mean like Eric?'

'No, stupid.' The wine and the intimate exchanges were liberating. They both laughed out loud. Gina added in a low voice, 'I call it my little beast.'

'How extremely apt.' Sam smiled again. 'But from now on, I shall call mine Eric.'

'You said this was a serious conversation, Sam.'

'It is. But Eric is far more useful to me than some of the men I've had the misfortune to entertain as lovers. And he's given me far more pleasure.'

'They haven't all given you orgasms?'

'My lovers have been a mixed bunch. How about you?'

'The same,' Gina said. 'Some very good, some very bad.'

They had become serious again.

Sam said, 'Usually, the good ones would provide me with a climax or six before they had theirs.'

'Six?'

'Some were very good. Sometimes it was more. The most I can remember having at any one time was eleven over a rather pleasant three hours.'

'What happened then?'

'I fell asleep.'

'I'm not surprised,' Gina said. 'I've had five or six but never reached double figures. If I did, I don't think I'd be able to walk afterwards.'

'I didn't try,' Sam said. 'I fell asleep.'

Gina smiled but carried on being serious.

'Most of the good lovers I've had knew how to touch me, how to give me orgasms. Sometimes while they were inside me. There have been occasions when I have climaxed without that stimulation, but they've been rare.'

Sam said, 'How about Hugo?'

Gina took refuge in the glass of wine but she knew it was truth time. She put the glass down.

'Hugo has never knowingly given me an orgasm.'

'I'm sorry.'

She shrugged.

'He gets aroused. Particularly since I started telling him stories. But he doesn't know how to make me come. The thing is, he excites me. I love the man – especially when he's naked. He really excites me. Sends me wild, if you like. But when he takes his clothes off, he doesn't lose his inhibitions. They're still there. They make him nervous, I know, but they make me nervous as well.'

Gina paused and licked her lips.

'We've never attempted oral sex. I wouldn't know how to suggest it to him. I certainly couldn't just go down on him without invitation. You know what you said about things becoming a habit? Once they become a habit, it is difficult to change. Well, that's what's happened to us.

'Hugo likes sex. His journal shows he does. I can tell he does. He shakes, sometimes, when he just touches me. Maybe he thinks I come. I mean, sometimes I make noises because he excites me and maybe he thinks that's it. But it isn't. His orgasm comes too quickly and I'm usually left high and dry and waiting for an opportunity to do it myself.'

'I know. I know.' Sam reached across the table and held her hand. 'We're a sad pair, aren't we? I have an absentee husband and you have one who might as well be.'

'No. I never want him to be absent. I still love him, Sam.'

Her friend smiled.

'For better or for worse? I know what you mean.' She released her hand and picked up the pieces of paper. 'But perhaps this is your way out. Perhaps this is salvation time.'

'How?'

'He wants to hear how it really happened. What your lovers did. So tell him and tell him the details of how they

64

made you come. Make him want to satisfy you, as they did.'

Gina nodded. She felt better for talking to her friend. The future looked more promising. She hoped the optimism wouldn't wear off with the wine.

Sam held up the photocopies.

'May I keep these?'

Gina had momentary doubts. Would she be compounding a disloyalty if she allowed her friend to keep them? On the other hand, where would she keep them if she took them home? What if Hugo found them?

'Keep them safe,' Gina said.

'Of course. I'll take them home with me. Will you bring me the next episode?'

'Do you think there will be one?'

'I'm sure of it.'

'I'll bring it.'

'Good.' Sam gave a soft smile. 'I'll read these again in bed.'

'Alone?'

'No, with a friend.'

Gina was puzzled.

'Which friend?'

'A girl's best,' Sam said, 'Eric.'

Chapter 8

Gina put down the *Daily Mail* and stared at *The Times*. Behind it, her husband ate a slice of granary toast. He crunched precisely.

He also looked precise, in his Paul Smith suit and Christian Dior tie. She had advised him on the suit and tie, insisting her flair and his tradition could be satisfactorily combined. They had, and now she chose most of his clothes.

Gina was fresh from the shower and wore only a white silk peignoir. Alongside his elegance, she felt slightly wanton.

'I'm thinking of going back to work,' she said.

'Mmm.'

He continued crunching and reading.

'Would you mind if I did?'

Asking a question gained his attention. He swallowed the toast.

'If you did what?'

'Went back to work.'

He stared in surprise.

'You want to go back to work?'

'I've been thinking about it for a while.'

'Doing what?'

'Public relations.'

He folded the newspaper and put it down.

'Do you still want to?'

'Yes. I was good.'

'I thought you were bored. That's why you stopped. Because you were bored.'

'I stopped because you asked me to stop when we got married.'

He looked puzzled.

'I didn't ask you to stop.'

'You suggested it, Hugo.'

'Did I? I thought you wanted to. You said it was boring.'

'I wanted to please you.' She smiled. 'It probably was boring at the time. Everything gets boring at some time.'

He was nonplussed, as if he had assumed too much. Her smile grew wider. He looked too precise to be nonplussed.

'So would you mind?' she said. 'If I got a job?'

'No, of course not. If that's what you want. Will you be able to?'

She laughed.

'Well, thank you for your confidence.'

'No, I'm sorry.' He was embarrassed. 'I didn't mean that. Of course you'll be able to.'

'Two years is a long time to be away but I still have contacts. Anyway, I'm still only thinking about it. I wanted to know what you thought.'

'If that's what you want, fine.' He smiled tentatively. 'Is marriage so boring?'

'You know it's not that. I thought about it the other day when I was with Sam. She was dashing back to the office to make editorial decisions and I was going to Harrods food hall. It occurred to me that I was just a lady who lunched. A lady who did not do a great deal else.'

'You make me happy.'

She laughed and reached across the table to touch his hand.

'It's mutual. But it would be nice to face a different kind of challenge, occasionally, other than whether to buy the Jasper Conran or the Cerutti.'

'Buy them both.'

'If I buy them both, that's even less of a challenge.'

'I suppose it is.' He smiled, sympathetically. 'I understand, darling. You have a good mind. It's right that you should want to use it.'

'So you have no objections?'

'None. As long as it doesn't entail you flying around the world and leaving me alone at home.'

'I wouldn't do that.' She thought of Sam and Brian's marriage that was often separated by several thousand miles. 'If I decide to go back into PR, and I still haven't, I thought I'd freelance. Maybe a few days a week.'

'Whatever you want to do.'

Gina was pleased at his reaction and pleased that she had actually got round to broaching the subject. By discussing it with Hugo, she had advanced it from an idea to a possibility. But it was still a possibility that deserved a lot more thought. As did the journal.

Gina wondered if he had added any more. He had had the opportunity the previous evening and this morning, for he was always an early riser.

When he went to the clinic in Harley Street, she went into the study and took the journal from the desk. He had completed more pages. She sat and stared at the new entry without reading it, anxious and curious at the same time. She took a deep breath, as if preparing to dive in at the deep end of a swimming pool, and began.

She read of her husband's excitement when he found her lying on the bed. Of how he had fantasized, as she had done, of being both her uncle and an intruder: a burglar who had found her by chance and had been unable to resist taking her.

His fantasy had developed other strands. It had placed Archie Tindall in the apartment. All red hair and fat belly, as Sam had described him. Hugo had placed Archie in the apartment by sending him on an errand. Instead, Archie had found an unconscious Gina. The sight had overcome his gentlemanly reservations and he had fucked her.

Those words again. Potent as ever, even in a silent fantasy come true.

The descriptions were vivid but the perspective was different. Her husband's arousal was obvious, not just on the evening of consummation but when he was writing the journal. She noted how the handwriting changed, how the letters became bigger with impatience, how the words sprawled in excitement.

Gina's mouth went dry. Her excitement was like an electric current. The writing stopped abruptly at the end of the paragraph. Two lines below, another paragraph started, the writing controlled, the content a summation, a conclusion of love where before there had been rampant lust. He had ended with the hope of a continuation of the stories in the future.

There could be only one explanation. Her husband had been so aroused by recounting what had happened that he had had to break off to calm himself down. Her eyes closed as she imagined him masturbating.

She took the journal to the bedroom and undressed. The muscles in her abdomen flickered, or was that imagination?

She wanted to rush but made herself take her time, kept the urgency at arm's length, fingertip length. She lay upon the bed naked and opened the journal and read again the final paragraphs, imagined her husband's excitement, imagined how he had relieved it, and, when the urgency became too intense, her fingers stole down across her stomach to the hungry little beast between her legs and she found her own relief.

The correct circumstances that would allow another incident to take place did not occur for four days. Gina and Hugo went to an informal bistro near the apartment and she allowed him to ply her with drink. On the way home, they called into a wine bar and she had more.

In the lift on the way up to their second floor home, she put her arms around him and kissed him.

'You're very handsome. Do you know that?' she said.

'You're very drunk. Do you know that?' he responded, more hopefully than accurately.

'I think you're right,' she said.

He had presented her with a role and she had accepted.

It was not all she had accepted. Gina realised she had entered the entire charade with her husband. That she had accepted his bizarre way of expanding their relationship.

During the evening, she had drunk more than she would have done normally so that the charade could continue. Her husband seemed to become bolder in direct proportion to her own impairment as a result of alcohol.

But Gina knew better than to drink too much. There was a difference between pleasant intoxication and oblivion. She had achieved intoxication and pretended it was deeper than it really was. In the process, the wine had emboldened her. There had been times when she had been on the brink of confessing that she knew about the journal.

Almost. She almost said she knew that Hugo knew she knew but, as she considered it, she laughed at herself because it would sound too much like a schoolgirl conundrum. It was better left unsaid at this stage. Better to play the game and allow Hugo to continue his experimentation.

If she were to unmask his pretensions now she might destroy what had already been achieved. If it had been strange, it had also been pleasurable. The journal was a deception to which they were both party and the unspoken secret made the encounters it inspired more tempting. Besides, there was more she wished to achieve before they could throw the book away.

But no, she would never throw it away. It made such fascinating bedtime reading.

When they reached the apartment, they went straight to the bedroom. By the time she had visited the bathroom, Hugo was in bed. Gina switched off the light and walked across the room. She dropped the white silk peignoir from her shoulders and hesitated, naked, as if lost.

'What is it?' he said.

His voice was huskier than before.

'My nightdress. Oh well, never mind. It's hot.'

She let him look at her nakedness in the dim light a moment longer before slipping beneath the sheet. They lay apart but she judged she had drunk enough wine to blatantly move against him and she rolled onto her side.

He was naked, as always. Her knee slid over his thigh, her breasts pushed against his chest, the curls of her pubis rubbed against his hip. The contact excited her. It roused the little beast. The beast wanted rubbing and she rubbed him gently against Hugo's hip. Her knee nudged his penis. It was erect.

Hugo stroked her hair from her face and kissed her forehead.

'I love you,' he said.

'I love you, too.'

He shifted onto his side and his erection lay against her stomach. Her face nestled into his shoulder and he kissed her neck.

'I love you so much,' he said. 'Sometimes it's difficult to tell you.' His voice cracked. 'You excite me, Gina. You excite me so much.'

He continued to kiss her neck and his hand moved down her body, over the curve of her hips onto her thigh, then onto her bottom. It stayed there and he felt her flesh.

'Do you remember you told me about Uncle Bernard? On holiday in Portugal?'

'Yes. I remember.'

'That excited me. It made me jealous and it made me love you more. It made me want to protect you. To keep you for myself.'

He kissed her again and she murmured her appreciation.

'Tell me another story. Something true. Something that happened.' His mouth nuzzled her ear. 'Did Uncle Bernard do anything else?'

'No. Nothing else happened with Uncle Bernard.'

'Then something else. Someone else. Tell me what they did?'

'If I do, you'll think I've been a bad girl.'

'No, I won't. It's all in the past. You were a different person then. Now you're my wife. I want you to share the past with me. Tell me, Gina. Tell me something from the past.'

Gina had rehearsed the story she would tell but she knew Hugo liked to persuade her.

'I could tell you what happened when I was seventeen.'

'Yes.' His voice was a husky whisper. 'Tell me what happened when you were seventeen.'

'All right. If you're sure?'

'I'm sure.'

She sighed.

'I don't know where to begin.'

She knew where to begin. But Hugo liked to prompt and she could not make it sound as if the story had been prepared.

'Just begin.'

'There was a boy, a young man. My parents didn't approve of him. Billy was older than me. He had a big old car. But they didn't like me going out with him. They didn't trust him. They didn't want me to associate with him.'

Gina paused, as if searching for the right words.

'What happened?' Hug said.

His hand squeezed her buttocks and his erection pressed hot against her stomach.

'My parents used my cousin as a chaperone. Peter was sixteen. He was staying with us. One evening, I said Billy was taking me to the cinema. My parents didn't approve but instead of trying to stop me, they said my cousin Peter would go with us.'

'Your cousin went with you?'

His erection lost a little of its heat and his hand faltered on her bottom.

'Yes. He sat in the back of the car. We went to the cinema but we left when the film started. Billy drove into the country and parked the car. He kissed me but I was nervous and embarrassed because Peter was in the back. So Billy made us all change places. Peter sat in the front seat and Billy and I got in the back. He told Peter to keep looking ahead. To ignore what was happening in the back.'

Gina paused again and licked Hugo's neck. His penis had regained its heat and his hand quivered on her flesh.

'What happened?' he demanded.

'Billy started kissing me. He groped me. His hands went over my breasts.'

Hugo's hand moved over her breasts.

'I wore a dress with buttons down the front and he opened them and pushed the dress off my shoulder. He pulled my breasts from my bra. I tried to object but I didn't want to make too much noise because of my cousin. Besides, Billy was big and strong. I couldn't have resisted.'

Her husband grunted and his mouth covered hers. His tongue invaded. She tasted his passion. Their mouths broke apart.

'Go on,' he said.

'He sucked my breasts. He pulled the dress open and sucked my breasts.'

Hugo's head went down and he sucked her breasts. Her hips arched against him. The head of his penis rubbed accidentally against her little beast. She moaned.

'While he sucked my breasts he put his hand up my skirt. He touched my bottom. Yes, like that. I couldn't stop him. Then I noticed the eyes in the rearview mirror. The eyes of my cousin Peter. He was looking ahead, as Billy had told him, but straight into the rearview mirror. He was watching us.'

Hugo re-surfaced.

'Peter was watching you?'

'Yes. He was watching Billy suck my breasts. He was watching me squirm about. He was watching Billy put his hand up my skirt.'

Her husband groaned and rubbed his penis against her. She opened her legs and moved her hips to attract attention but he would not be rushed.

'What happened then?'

'Billy lay me along the seat and pushed my skirt up to my waist. I kept saying no but he ignored me. He kissed me to stop me saying no and he pulled my panties down with one hand. He pulled them down around my thighs. He sucked my breasts again, and over his shoulder I could see Peter watching. He had half turned in the seat and was looking straight at us. His face was red, his eyes wide.'

'Was he excited?'

'Yes. He was excited.'

'Were you excited?'

'Yes. I was excited, too.'

'But Billy had forced you?'

'He was stronger than me.'

'He forced you?'

'I wanted to be forced. I enjoyed it.'

Hugo groaned and dipped his head to suck her breasts again.

Gina said, 'Billy sucked them. Like that. And his hand went between my legs. Yes, there. I was wet and he put a finger inside.' She groaned as her husband pushed a finger into her vagina. 'Then another.' He put two inside her. 'He moved them in and out to make me wetter.' She moaned and moved her hips. 'I was so very wet.'

Her husband trailed his mouth upwards to her neck and over her face. His tongue found hers and they kissed. This was better than before. Hugo was more excited than before and was moving to her directions.

'What did he do then?'

'I was still protesting. Still trying to push his hands away. He was kneeling in the back of the car, leaning over me. He held my body down with his left arm across me. His left hand held a breast. His right hand was between my legs, his fingers inside me. He was fucking me with his fingers.'

Her husband groaned and did what she said Billy had done.

Gina said, 'Billy stopped sucking my breasts and knelt up. He smiled into my face, into my eyes, as he fucked me with his fingers. I remember, they made a noise as they went in and out.'

Hugo's fingers squelched in their rhythm.

'Then he took them out. He took his fingers out and rubbed me. There.'

Hugo slid his fingers out of her vagina and she reached between their bodies to guide them onto her clitoris.

'Yes,' she groaned. 'Just there. He knew how sensitive that was. He moved his fingers there, on the bud.' She closed her eyes and her head rolled back on the pillow. 'He kept doing it, doing it. He could feel me losing control.'

Now Gina was losing control. She moaned and her hips writhed. Hugo's fingers strayed and she put them back in place, held them in place.

'Just there. He kept doing it, making me moan.' She moaned. 'And my cousin watched and Billy kept smiling at me and his fingers kept doing it, kept doing it until, until . . . I came.'

Gina came, her body convulsing around her husband's hand. Her legs twitched, her shoulders rose from the bed.

Moans dribbled from her open mouth.

Hugo lay next to her, temporarily adrift. This was beyond his comprehension. He had never seen Gina react this way. He had never watched her have such a blatant and uncontrolled orgasm before.

As she recovered, she realised she had to re-immerse him in the story before he compared what he had just witnessed with previous moments of passion. Self-doubt might sap his libido if he thought he had previously been a failure.

'Billy made me come with his fingers while my cousin watched,' she said.

Hugo still looked puzzled and she kissed him.

'I lost control and I shook beneath his fingers and all the time he smiled. And all the time, my cousin watched.' She licked her lips. 'Billy said . . .'

Her voice became hoarse and she moved her face away and hid it in her husband's neck, a shy and seduced young girl afraid to continue.

'What did he say?' her husband demanded.

Lustful anticipation cleared any lingering doubts.

'He said he had done it for me, so I had to do it for him.'

'Done what?'

'Made me come. He said he had made me come, so I had to make him come.'

He kissed her neck and his hands moved over her body, gently, tenderly, reassuringly, telling her that he treasured her and loved her and wanted her to continue.

'And did you?' he whispered.

'Yes. I did.'

Chapter 9

This had surpassed her expectations. She had taught Hugo how to give her an orgasm.

The truth of what really happened in the back of the car had been slightly different. Billy had been too young to be a great lover. He had only been interested in achieving his own satisfaction.

He had been a handsome layabout, if the truth be known. A guitarist in a local rock band that was going nowhere. He had long black curly hair and wore denim and boots with heels that made him walk like a cowboy. He was lean and muscular, with piercing blue eyes and a mouth that could be cruel.

Gina had thought him delicious and dangerous. So had all her friends. That was one reason why she had gone out with him; to provoke their jealousy.

She and Billy had been chaperoned by her cousin Peter several times. It was a forlorn attempt by her parents to ensure she did not stray into the perceived evils of sex, drugs and rock and roll. If only they had known.

On the first occasion, the three of them had actually gone to the cinema where she and Billy had kissed and fumbled in the dark. Afterwards, they had gone straight home. But on the second or third occasion, they had gone to a pub in the town before Billy had parked the car. Their kisses had been more demonstrative and his hands had been more adventurous.

Her cousin had remained in the back of the car and had watched the silhouette of their heads and listened to the sounds of their mouths and the grunts they made as their hands touched sensitive areas.

Peter's presence had excited her. Having an audience excited her. It made her an actress.

Games again. In her mind, it had been another game, as most sex was a game. But however this one was played, her cousin's presence excited her.

She was no virgin and she was eager to please her boyfriend. He did not bring her to orgasm but she gained almost as much satisfaction by masturbating him and watching the changes in his face as her hands worked upon his penis. And all the time Peter watched their silhouettes from the back seat and listened to Billy's groans.

The third time they parked, Billy took the situation a step further. He pushed her head down into his lap and she took him in her mouth and fellated him. He came in her mouth and made a great deal of noise.

When she sat up, she looked into the back of the car at her cousin. Peter was in the corner, his legs drawn up, his hands in his lap. His eyes were wide and his lips trembled.

Gina and her cousin were physically alike. They shared the same features. At times, she felt she was looking into a mirror, at her male doppelganger. Did they still look the same after what she had just done? They probably did. Both stared wide-eyed and both had trembling lips.

She licked her lips and saw him shudder. The excitement

was better than an orgasm. The excitement was power to make men weak. She licked her lips again and smiled.

They all knew the situation could not continue, that the strain of the three-way secret was too intense to keep. They knew they were caught in a ritual that had to reach a conclusion. That it had to end.

The last time, Billy drove into the country and parked the car. This last time, they changed over, and her cousin sat in the front seat and she and her boyfriend sat in the back. It was a large car and the back seat was like a bed.

As always, they had parked without discussion about what was going to happen. They never discussed what was going to happen and, afterwards, they never discussed what had happened.

It was as if the sex was separate from life. They could discuss the subterfuge; prepare alibis as to where they would pretend they had been, but they never referred to where they had really been or what they had really done.

Sex was a secret and, Gina reflected, it was still a secret.

The last time.

Funnily enough, Gina had sensed it would be the last time as she sat in the back seat and exchanged looks with her cousin. Billy didn't know, and afterwards he had wanted it to continue. But she had known, as she sat in the back of the car, that they had reached the end of what they had together. She realised before they started their rituals that this would be the last time.

Her cousin had become a proper audience. He no longer had to be content with silhouettes. He leaned against the passenger door and stretched his legs across the front seats and stared into the back of the car, stared onto his own private stage, and waited for the performance to begin.

Gina remembered the expectancy in his face. She remembered deciding, on this last occasion, that she would give him a performance to remember.

Billy also reacted to Peter's unrestricted view. When they started kissing, he opened her dress as if they were making a film. He slipped it from her shoulders and trapped her arms, slipped down the straps of her bra and pulled the cups down to reveal her breasts.

Her breasts were large, even then. Billy had released them, mauled them with his hands and then sat back to allow Peter to see them, naked and quivering, the nipples erect. Everything he had done at first had been with Peter in mind and Gina had enjoyed being the star of the show.

Afterwards, she realised Billy had been playing games of his own. Power games.

Look what I can do to her. Watch my power. Watch me bend her body to my whim. Watch me make her do anything I desire.

Afterwards, she also realised Billy had got it wrong.

Gina was the one with the power. It was her body that Billy craved and that her cousin watched with wide, begging eyes. It was she who had made Billy's penis go so hard he found it painful when she touched him. It was she who made him come three times as they grunted and moaned and moved in the confined space, their bodies sweating, filling the car with heat and smells of sex.

Billy stripped her. He kissed her body all over. For the first time he kissed her between her legs. It was the first time anyone had kissed her between her legs. His mouth and tongue were inexpert but, as his fingers had already opened her vagina and made her wet and as the situation was already highly charged, it had the desired effect.

She came.

The orgasm surprised and embarrassed her. She was not used to having orgasms with boys but then, she was not used to having a mouth sucking at her vagina. She hid the orgasm, successfully, but it made her languid and pliable. It made her want to reward Billy.

For two hours, Peter watched without complaint. For two hours she moved to Billy's direction as he put into practice the fantasies he had imagined. His penis was large and uncircumcised. But that first time it was so hard it was sensitive and needed only the gentlest of caresses. He lay back across the seat and pushed down her head.

Gina held his penis around the base and let her nipples brush the tip. Billy groaned as if in pain. She looked up, through the strands of her dishevelled hair, at her cousin. Peter was staring, not at her, but at the penis she held. His face was set. She could tell from the slight movements of his body that he was masturbating.

His eyes met hers. She smiled and licked her lips. He gulped and his eyes darted from her mouth to the bulbous head of Billy's penis, as if trying to bridge the gap. Gina parted her lips, dipped her head and took it into her mouth.

She sucked and Billy cried out. She rolled the foreskin back with her tongue and boiled the glans in her saliva and he came without control. She held it tightly in both hands and swallowed his sperm; quick swallows, one after the other as the salty liquid spurted into her mouth.

When he finished, she released the softening penis and looked back at her cousin. He was no longer watching. His head lay back against the seat and his eyes stared sightlessly at the roof of the car. He, too, had come.

The feeling of power stayed with her for the rest of the

evening and nothing could match that first orgasm she had sucked from Billy, even though he had sex with her in a variety of ways. No, not sex. He fucked her.

Gina moaned at the memory. He fucked her and, sometimes, fucking was better than making love.

Hugo said, 'How did you make him come?'

Gina returned to her alternative version and mixed reality with imagination.

'I masturbated him.'

'Do it,' he said.

He moved slightly away from her and she reached between them and took hold of his erection. Her finger and thumb took a firm grip around the base and the palm of her other hand flitted over the sensitive head. This was uncircumcised, like Billy's.

Where are you now, Billy?

Are you still fucking in the back of cars?

Her husband shuddered.

'That's good,' he whispered. 'You do it so well.'

They kissed and his hands went over her breasts.

'That's what Billy did. He touched my breasts. Squeezed them, felt them. And all the time Peter watched. Watched me masturbating Billy, watched his hands upon me.'

'He just watched?'

'I couldn't see, but I think he was masturbating, too. As he watched.'

Hugo shuddered.

'Did Billy come like this?'

'No.'

'What did he do?' His voice was hoarse. 'Did he fuck you?'

It would have been easy to say yes but Gina wanted to keep the momentum going. She wanted to reward her husband for giving her an orgasm and to take him a step further.

'No. He didn't fuck me.' She sensed his disappointment. 'He did something else.'

She nuzzled his neck again to hide her face.

'What did he do? Tell me? What did he do?'

'He made me do something else.'

Her husband had almost lost his voice. The unspeakable act that had occurred had restored his vibrancy. She felt he might come at any moment in her hands.

'What did he make you do?'

Gina slid lower in the bed, taking the sheet with her, and kissed his chest. She turned her face so that she could breath the words up to him.

'He took hold of my head. Yes, like that. And he pushed it down.' Hugo began to push and hesitated. She kissed his stomach and licked his navel. She gazed up his body and said, 'He pushed my head all the way down. Until his prick was in my face.'

Hugo gasped. He sounded as if he were being tortured.

'And then what did he do?'

'He put it in my mouth. He put his prick in my mouth. He made me suck him. He came in my mouth.'

Hugo still held her head but the strength seemed to have gone from his arms. His erection jumped in her hand. Gina turned her face towards his groin and slid further down. She pushed the sheet with her feet until it dropped from the end of the bed.

His hands still held her head. An impassive token of the game, but she had gone too far to stop now. At least his penis had not lost its strength. It pulsed. She could feel the pulse in her hand, she could see the pulse in the veins that powered it.

Gina was filled with a delicious feeling of depravity at being about to fellate her husband for the first time. She had taken many pricks into her mouth but this occasion was special. Her stomach tingled and her little beast needed attention. She held Hugo's penis in her left hand and slipped her right down between her legs, out of sight of her husband. She looked up the bed once more.

In a small voice, she said, 'He made me do this.'

Gina opened her mouth and took the head of the penis inside. She did it softly and, at first, simply held it in the pressure of her lips. Hugo sighed as if she had released all the air from his body and his fingers delved gently into her hair.

She gulped for saliva and licked the end with her tongue. The fingers of her right hand rubbed the little beast between her legs. Her first orgasm might be the strongest but it had prepared her for more and the beast trembled and promised it would be soon.

Hugo groaned and his fingers gripped her hair more firmly.

Gina sucked and dipped her head and took half the length of the penis into her mouth so that it bulged her cheek.

He whimpered. She sensed he was at her mercy. He was incapable of thought or speech. Her fingers moved over the beast of her clitoris and felt that her lust was in tune with his. She moved her head up and down upon the shaft, all the time milking the base with her fingers and thumb, and his whimper became a moan that became a groan that became a yell and, suddenly and uncontrollably, he came. His hands flopped by his side and his hips shook and he spurted his sperm into her mouth in an endless stream, and she came, too, as a reaction to the strength of his orgasm.

Afterwards, Hugo remained lying on his back and she knew he did not know how to react. It would be better not to make him react. She moved back up the bed, pulling the sheet with her, and kissed his neck.

She whispered, 'You are so good, darling. So strong, so exciting. So understanding.' She kissed him again. 'I love you.'

'I love you, too. So much.'

Gina rolled onto her side, her back to him but close enough so that their bodies touched. His thigh lay immobile against her buttocks. She made no demands for affection or forgiveness because none were necessary in fantasy. She did not intrude upon his thoughts.

Tomorrow, or the next day, she would be able to discover them by reading the journal. Their discreet dialogue would continue safely, at a distance, and she would be able go gauge whether the pace she was setting was acceptable.

She would discover what he thought of unspeakable acts such as fellatio and of the power of the orgasm that had rocked her upon his fingers. She would find out if he wanted to continue to learn about sex and his own potential, or if his sensibilities were so offended he was ready to say enough is enough.

But Gina had no doubts as to what he would decide. He enjoyed sex too much to stop now. If his sensibilities were offended, he would adjust them. He would find reasons to continue.

Sam had declared the truism of the situation, the first time they discussed the merits and morality of telling stories. Men liked the rude bits, the dirty bits. Hugo liked to hear her say fuck. Now he had also heard her say suck. He would want her to say it again, and do it again.

Gina licked the remnants of his sperm from her teeth and swallowed it. What would Sam say when she told her? *If* she told her? But she would not have to tell her. Hugo would write it in the journal and Sam could read about it over lunch.

Chapter 10

Gina half expected to be awakened during the night by Hugo making fresh demands, if not for more stories then physical demands upon her body. She was almost disappointed that he hadn't. Perhaps if she had told him the full story . . .

Even now she did not like to think of it except obliquely, allowing the memory into her mind in the wake of other recollections. It had been a long time since she had thought about what had happened in the back of Billy's car.

Teenage indiscretions. Everybody had them lurking somewhere in the past. But at the time they had not been indiscretions, they had been pulsating sexual adventures. Once again, she wondered if it would be possible to recapture that same intensity, when it had all been so new.

She and her cousin had been alike, facially and in nature. When she was seventeen and he sixteen, experience and adulthood had not yet lined their faces or dictated patterns of behaviour. Now they were a lot less alike. He had put on weight and lost much of his hair. He had also lost his sense of wonder and adventure in the finance houses of the City.

He was married and had two children. His wife and the children lived in the country and he saw them at weekends.

During the week he stayed at his apartment in the Barbican but his wife never had cause to suspect infidelity. Peter was now far too involved in making money to contemplate an affair on the side. It would get in the way of his schedule. His only seducer was money.

But back then he had been interested in sex. Back then he had been a good-looking boy filled with excessive lust. Some boys liked sport, Peter liked sex. Perhaps she and Billy had been the cause of his obsession.

After that last time in the car, the tensions had continued when she and Peter went home. They had exchanged the minimum of small talk with her parents, presented their alibis and had them accepted. They had gone to bed as soon as politely possible.

Gina had been unable to sleep. She had been unwilling to sleep. She did not want the memory of what had happened to fade and kept re-running it in her mind while her fingers played between her legs, holding her emotions on the high slopes of desire without quite tipping her over into orgasm.

Sometime in the night, after her parents had gone to bed and the house was silent, Peter came into her room. He was hesitant and unsure. He stood by the bed in his pyjamas and she reached out from the bed and held his hand. They didn't speak, they didn't have to. Words would have been an intrusion.

They stared at each other and she remembered staring into his eyes as she crouched in the back of the car and prepared to take Billy in her mouth. Peter's look had not been one of accusation then and was not one of recrimination now. His look was exactly the same: it was lustful.

Not naked lust but confused lust. His body had been aroused by the sight of a girl having sex with a man and his body had not acknowledged that the girl was his cousin, no matter what reservations his mind might have had.

Gina knew they had broken taboos that night, for she, too, had been aroused by the presence of another male. The fact that it had been her cousin had added a piquancy to the thrill.

Now he stood by her bed and held her hand and shook with desire and words were the last thing either of them wanted or needed.

Gina pulled back the bedclothes in invitation and he got in beside her. They pulled the blankets up and hid from the conventions of the outside world. They faced each other and smelled each other's breath. She touched him over the front of his pyjama trousers and felt his erection and he yelped like a puppy and shook more fiercely.

She opened the pyjamas and took hold of his penis and felt as if she were touching herself. He lay with one hand trapped beneath his side. The other touched her breasts through the cotton nightdress. She squeezed his penis and he closed his eyes and his hand froze as if he might explode at any moment.

Her free hand took his free hand between their bodies and placed it between her thighs. She wore no panties and she was wet from playing with herself. She placed his fingers in the mouth of the valley, pressed them in the right place and moved subtly against them and breathed heavily to make him aware that his touch was effective.

He continued to stare into her eyes and she directed his fingers deeper between her legs so that he could discover her vagina. He tested its dimensions, probed inside with two fingers, and allowed them to be led back to the little beast of her clitoris.

Again she moved and moaned to indicate the spot upon which he should concentrate. He nodded imperceptibly. He learned quickly and his fingers were dextrous and fluid. With great surprise, Gina came within a minute.

She gasped, mouth open, eyes staring into his, and he continued using his fingers and she came again.

When she regained her composure, she stopped him doing it a third time.

This was wrong. This could not be allowed to develop. This was substitute sex that had arisen from deliberate flaunting of society's rules, of breaking those taboos that made it so exciting, except that the idea was more exciting than the reality.

Gina regretted inviting Peter into her bed but still felt compassion for him. She also felt the strength of his erection in her hand. He had done it for her: she was obliged to do it for him. Do it quickly and get it over. End this as she knew the meetings with Billy had ended because they could go no further.

After all, how far could they go?

She used both her hands upon his penis, masturbating him swiftly and causing him to open his mouth in a silent moan. He freed his trapped arm and both his hands touched her beneath the bedclothes, feeling her buttocks and her breasts, feeling for the first time in lust what he had only previously imagined.

Then his hands were on her shoulders, in her hair.

Please don't try to kiss me, she thought, but he didn't. He was pushing down on her head, wanting her to go beneath the bedclothes, to go down and take him in her mouth as she had taken Billy.

Gina shook her head firmly. She masturbated him more

urgently and felt his pulse quicken. There was disappoint-ment and anger in his eyes. He looked as if he had been betrayed. Had she led him to expect too much?

He pushed again and this time she went beneath the bedclothes. As she neared his groin, she could smell him in the hot and confined space. She guessed he had mastur-bated in his own bed before coming to hers. But now she was committed and she must complete the act as quickly as possible. Get it over with, for now and for ever.

Her hands continued to work on his penis, around its base and along its length. Her head moved in the darkness closer to the glans which she had released from the fore-skin. The smell was stronger here, beneath the blankets, and she lost sense of distance for the penis nudged her cheek.

How had she allowed it to go this far? She opened her mouth and allowed her cousin's penis to slip inside. She sucked and he came, as quickly as that. His hips bucked and he spurted into her mouth and she swallowed.

As soon as his tremors ceased, she began to move back up the bed. Amazingly, now that the lust had gone from him, she felt it had freed her of commitments and even guilt. She again felt sisterly towards him. She paused and fastened his pyjama trousers.

Her head broke from the cover of the blankets and he rolled away from her and got out of bed. He paused with his back towards her, his hands by his side. Once more, she reached out from the bed and took hold of a hand and squeezed it. He squeezed back. They were once more cousins.

Peter left as silently as he had arrived. Providing relief for him had closed the circle. This episode, she decided, was now properly ended. Now she was able to sleep.

In the morning, Hugo did not disturb her and she awoke alone. Did he want to avoid her? She wandered the apartment in her peignoir.

'Hugo?'

'In here.'

Gina opened the study door. He sat at the desk, the journal open before him and a fountain pen in his hand.

'You didn't wake me,' she said.

'You looked peaceful.' He smiled. 'I let you sleep.'

She smiled back, reassured.

'Do you want coffee?' she said.

'No thank you. I have to leave soon.'

'I'll take my coffee into the shower. Shout before you go.'

'I will.'

Gina used the bathroom and showered. Her reflection in the mirror suggested she had had more to drink the previous night than she had thought. Still, nothing a little make-up could not put right. If there was ever a war, she thought, she could be a camouflage artist.

Hugo came into the bathroom to say goodbye while she was still applying her personal camouflage.

'What a memory to take to work,' she said.

She meant her face, but was aware of the double entendre.

'You are beautiful,' Hugo said. 'You are always beautiful.' He kissed her cheek. 'I'll call.'

'I'll be out for lunch. I'm seeing Sam.'

'Drunk again?'

'We never get drunk. We get high on each other's

company.' She smiled. 'It's like being back at school.'

'You must tell me about it sometime.' He, too, could use double meanings. ''Bye.'

He left the room before she could see his face. He was getting bolder. She heard the outside door of the apartment open and close and stared at herself in the mirror. Did she have the control to complete her make-up or would the temptation of the journal prove too strong?

Damn it! She had never been one to frustrate temptation. She went into the study.

Gina sat behind the desk, took the book from its drawer and began to read the latest entry:

I started this journal as a record of what I hoped would be my emotional and sexual advancement. I also said there would be confessions. Now seems the right time to make one.

Sex scares me. Written coldly like this, it seems a rather silly statement. But I am married to a beautiful woman whom I know is vastly experienced and I am intimidated in her presence. Always I need to feel in a superior position before I can react with the passion I wish to show.

When I finally tell her of my fears, as I will one day, I hope she will forgive me for the way I have manufactured what, in essence, is my education.

Perhaps I am simply a fool who concentrated on medicine because of imagined inadequacies. I am certainly a fool for missing out until now on the wonderful experiences I have enjoyed in the last few weeks. Sex still scares me and my lack of knowledge inhibits me. But, by God, sex thrills me.

Last night went beyond my imagination. Of course I know of fellatio. I have read of it, heard of it, listened to men talk about it. It is both a poor word and a useful word. Cock-sucking is more to the point, more guttural, more basic, more arousing. But fellatio allows one to think of it almost as a medical term, it allows cock-sucking to be mentioned in polite conversation, except that cock-sucking does not belong in polite conversation.

Simply writing it down, thinking it in my head, gives me an erection. Can my repression be cured by words and vulgarity? Why do I love to use such words, in my head and here, in secret, in this journal?

In a while I will recount in detail what happened last night. I have to be careful because doing so will, I know, arouse me again and Gina may awaken at any time. Gina still sleeps, by the way. There were times during the night I wanted to throw myself upon her and ravish her, when I wanted to make her do again what she did last night, when I wanted . . .

But already I am getting too excited. If she only knew the power she has over me!

Two things I need to mention about last night. Gina performed fellatio upon me. She sucked my cock. She went down and took my cock into her mouth and sucked it until . . .

This is more difficult than I imagined. Even dressed in a suit and sitting at a desk I can hardly control myself. The pen shakes in my hand.

But she performed fellatio, an act of which I had heard, an act I knew was practised. But how widely? By whom? I had learned in my youth not to take seriously what other young men claimed. The way they talked, fellatio was something every girl did and every man expected by right. Not so. I can imagine it is a practice that some women would abhor and I had judged it to be an act that was offered rather than demanded.

It could be Gina would have offered to perform the act before but was put off by my priggish behaviour. It is a sad fact of life but I know my faults and liabilities. I can be particularly priggish when my inexperience is threatened. That such pride should get in the way when such delights were waiting to be sampled!

But at last, by manipulation and too much wine, we have breached that barrier. Now I am torn with doubt again. How often is this practised? Every time a couple makes love? Or on special occasions? Should it ever be demanded?

I shudder at the story she told, of how she was forced to perform the act. God, how I wish I had been that young man with the confidence to demand. How I wish I had been her cousin and been able to watch.

To the second point, and one of which I am ashamed.

Almost by accident, Gina showed me how this boyfriend had given her an orgasm with his fingers. Watching her squirm and heave when she climaxed was a revelation. Surely, this was not the first time I have given her a climax?

I understood that orgasm was intrinsic with the act of sex. That the clitoris was stirred by the very act of penetration and the rhythm of sex. I assumed that each time we had sex Gina had a climax. And yet, watching her writhe beneath my fingers last night, tells me I was wrong.

How thoughtless I have been in the two years we have been married. I have been so wrapped up in my own doubts that I have been unable to give my wife satisfaction. A wife who has obviously known great satisfaction in the past.

I look forward to more of her stories and, in my own way, of progressing to the point where I need no longer keep this journal. But I have discovered that I do need education if I am to benefit from what Gina tells me. I need to study the theory of sexual experience before I can hope to be a complete practitioner.

But where does one get the books, the texts, the manuals for such study? They are not the sort of thing I can ask my secretary to obtain for me. I shall endeavour, nonetheless, and now that certain secrets have been unlocked, perhaps I might learn how to reciprocate to my beautiful wife without causing her offence.

I refer, of course, to cunnilingus.

This time my trepidation is not entirely based upon Gina's reaction. In part, it is based upon my own. What if I make an attempt at this act and find it repulsive? Except that is not possible. I love everything about my wife, particularly the smell of her upon my fingers. Surely, this act will be an act of worship and one I need to make. But that is for the future.

Before then, I need to study my subject. Would Gina, for instance, be repulsed at my fantasies? Are they, in fact, totally male fantasies? Or do women also dream of sexual exploits beyond the ordinary?

But now, I must recount the story Gina told me last night and the consequences it inspired.

Chapter 11

Sam was already at their table in the restaurant when Gina arrived. Mario greeted her with effusive warmth. Perhaps he had the restaurant wired for sound and had tape-recorded their intimate conversations?

Gina smiled sweetly at him and wondered when was the last time he had had his prick sucked. One of these days, she might ask him.

Her ebulliance surprised her, or was it anticipation at being able to shock Sam with more disclosures? All this sex was making her take a greater interest in life in general. Was that why she was considering going back to work?

Mario escorted her between the other diners and pulled back the chair for her to sit. The two women exchanged looks instead of a greeting. Sam poured red wine into Gina's glass.

'I almost called you,' she said.

'Why?'

'You know why. How's the journal?'

Gina smiled.

'Coming along nicely.'

'There's more?'

'Yes. There's more.'

They stared at each other.

Sam said, 'For God's sake, Gina, don't make me beg. Have you brought it?'

Gina laughed and opened her satchel and took out the photocopied sheets. She hesitated before handing them over.

'Shouldn't we order, first?'

'I've lost my appetite. Give me.'

Gina gave her the pages.

'Well, I'm going to order.' She attracted Mario's attention. 'What do you want?'

'What?'

She was already reading.

'What do you want to eat?'

'I'll have the tagliatelle.'

'No starter?'

'I'm not hungry. Let me read.'

'Amazing. We may have found the diet that really works: sex. But how do we market it?'

'Shut up, Gina.'

Gina shut up and ordered. Her own appetite was fine but Sam was too distracted to eat. Her friend pushed the pasta around her plate for a while before abandoning it to read the pages from the journal a second time.

Eventually, when the plates had been cleared and the second bottle of wine opened, the two friends exchanged more relaxed looks.

Gina said, 'Well?'

'Amazing stuff.' Sam still had a blush on her cheeks from what she had read. 'I mean, perhaps it's because I'm reading about two people I know but, well, it's made me as horny as hell.'

'Really? I thought you had access to all manner of erotic literature.'

'It's not the same. I mean, this is real. This is written by hand, for Christ's sake. At times, a very shaky hand.'

'I'd noticed that, too.'

Sam raised an eyebrow.

'And did you notice how the handwriting steadied down again? Afterwards?'

'Yes.'

'Mmm.' Sam's eyes became dreamy for a moment. 'Do you think he . . . well . . . do you?'

'I'm damn sure he did,' Gina said. 'I know I did when I read it.'

'Did you?'

'Didn't you?' Gina said. 'When you took it home?'

Sam blushed and nodded.

'Yes, I did.' She glanced at the pages. 'Your stories are rather good. And the rest, well . . .'

Gina smiled. She also thought the stories were rather good and Hugo had expanded them extremely well. They were obviously vivid in his imagination. His descriptions of what they did together during and afterwards were equally vivid. Letting Sam read them was like inviting her into the bedroom to watch.

'Are they good enough to publish?' Gina said.

'Are you serious?'

'Probably not. But give me an opinion?'

'It depends where they lead. At the moment, you've only got an outline. But a few more chapters could give you the basis for a book.'

'Fact or fiction?'

'If you made it factual you could claim respectability and

sell more copies. You could become the British Nancy Friday.' Sam smiled. 'You could end up on all the television chat shows.'

'Talking about my sex life?'

'Talking about sex. Change the names in the journal and claim you used volunteers. That you set up the whole scheme as research. That you suggested to a couple who could not discuss sex openly together, to use the journal as a way of communicating.'

'A discreet dialogue?'

'Exactly.'

Gina smiled.

'You are developing this into a marketable commodity.'

'I suppose that's part of my job.' Sam chuckled. 'You could end up a sex therapist, Gina. An armchair expert. Have you ever done it in an armchair?'

'Don't you need qualifications?'

'To do it in an armchair?'

'To be a so-called expert.'

'You've hit the nail on the head. So-called expert. Have you seen them? On those late-night television shows? They are as charismatic as rice pudding. A good night in bed to them probably means cocoa and a *Woman's Own* knitting pattern. And that's just the men.'

Gina laughed and Sam continued.

'To talk about fucking you have to know how to fuck. At least you look as if you know how.'

'Are you calling me a tart?'

'Certainly not, darling. But a beautiful woman talking sex is far more convincing than an elderly professor with a bald head.'

'And I suppose that's just the women?'

'You're catching on, kid.'

'You are talking a load of nonsense, Sam.'

'Absolutely.' Sam grinned. 'But you might consider the possibility. This as research material, a couple of platitudinous chapters of sexual cant, and you as author, all adds up to a very marketable product.'

'What would Hugo say?'

'You would have to tell him first.'

'And when would I do that?'

'When he finishes the journal.'

'You think I should let it continue?' Gina said.

'Don't be facetious. It will continue. You want it to continue. You can dictate whatever situation you like and Hugo will play it out. You lucky girl.'

'Yes, I am, aren't I?'

Sam sipped wine and looked at her through lowered eyelashes.

'He'd never had his prick sucked?'

Gina coughed, embarrassed at the personal nature of the question. She glanced around the restaurant.

'No. He hadn't.'

'Mmmm.'

Sam looked dreamy.

'You lucky girl,' she said, again.

Now Gina blushed.

'I know.'

'And he's waiting to be taught to . . .?'

She leaned back in her chair and pointed less than discreetly at her thighs.

Gina coughed.

'You are beginning to sound envious.'

'I am envious. If he needs someone to practise on, give me a call.'

'Samantha!'

The use of her full name was an admonishment.

'Sorry.' She sipped more wine. 'Are you going to Roger's birthday party on Friday?'

'Yes, we are. Why?'

'So am I. I was just thinking, it'll be strange seeing the two of you together after reading this.'

'You mustn't let on that you know anything, Sam,' Gina warned.

'Of course not.' She smiled. 'Is Archie Tindall going?'

Gina laughed.

'Probably.'

'Let's hope Hugo doesn't hit him.'

'Hugo should be grateful. In a way, Archie started all this,' Gina said. 'Is Brian going?'

'He's away. I'll be flying solo.'

'No, you won't. You'll go with us. Our own little *ménage à trois*.'

'You had better not mention that to Hugo. It might give him ideas.'

The girls laughed, but Gina realised Sam was only too right.

Chapter 12

Roger Billington was a former male model turned actor who had been able to indulge his whims of fast women and fast cars rather than pursue a real career because of an inheritance from an uncle in Staffordshire whose company made chamber pots.

'Before uncle died I didn't have a pot to piss in,' he was fond of saying. 'Now I have hundreds.'

The pots were mainly exported to America and Australia and the company continued to prosper and provide a regular income, for which the notoriously profligate Roger was grateful. He was tall, blond, slim and handsome. His hair flopped over his forehead and he had a feminine habit of brushing it back with one hand. That was the only feminine habit he had.

Gina had known Roger before she met Hugo and had had a brief fling with him. They remained good friends although there was always a sexual frisson between them that she suspected Hugo was aware of.

The party was at his house in Belgravia to celebrate his fortieth birthday and promised to be hectic rather than refined. Hugo would be out of place.

Gina prepared for the party with unselfconscious erotic

intent. She put on pale blue underwear and tan stockings and paraded around the apartment on high heels. She was determined to set the tone for the evening.

The bra was designed to enhance her cleavage and its effect was impressive. The garter belt was deep cut. The straps that tautly held the stockings at front and rear, created archways of silk that framed her pubis and the curve of her bottom. The panties were a brief high-cut triangle that covered little and hinted at a great deal.

Underwear such as this was worn with men in mind. If a woman wanted to be comfortable, she would choose cotton briefs and pantyhose. But although worn for Hugo, it also had the effect of heightening Gina's awareness of her own sexuality.

In these circumstances, where there was a latent promise of adventure, the stockings, the high heels and the feel of the straps across her thighs, made her sensitive to any nuance of desire.

Because she was prepared for sex it made her more attuned to sex. Every glance she received at the party, every verbal exchange, would be interpreted differently because of what she wore beneath her dress and the way it focused her mind.

Hugo watched her surreptitiously. She felt his eyes following her and knew she was inciting his passion. She intended to continue to stoke it during the course of the evening.

Sam arrived by taxi from her apartment in St Katherine's Dock. Hugo let her in and she gave him a peck on the cheek. She looked stunning in a simple black shift dress and high heels. Gina watched from the other side of the living room, still in her underwear.

'I'm glad we're not competing,' Gina said. 'You look lovely.'

Her friend laughed.

'If you go like that you'll win all the prizes,' Sam said. 'How can you keep your hands off her, Hugo?'

'He has medical training,' Gina said.

The two girls embraced.

'Where did you get the underwear?' Sam said enviously. She looked at Hugo. 'A gift from an admirer?'

'A little shop I found near Sloane Square.'

'You must take me. See if they can do anything for my boobs.'

'I've told you before.' Gina caressed Sam's right breast in her palm. 'You have lovely breasts. Hasn't she, Hugo?'

Hugo gulped and concentrated on opening a bottle of champagne.

'Delightful,' he said.

'You wouldn't advise implants?' Sam asked.

Gina thought her friend might be tempted to suggest Hugo give her a physical examination here and now and restrained her with an arm around her waist.

'You don't need implants, Sam.' He coughed and poured the wine. 'You're perfectly proportioned.'

'What a genteel compliment,' Sam said.

The girls chatted and laughed together as if Hugo was not there and drank champagne while Gina pretended to complete her preparations. Sam help her into a long dark blue summer dress. It had a low-cut front that showed off her breasts and fluid lines that caressed her hips.

'What a beautiful dress,' said Sam.

'Bruce Oldfield.'

'But of course.'

'What's yours?'

Sam smirked and held her skirt like a little girl showing off at a party.

'Roman Road Market.'

'You could make sackcloth and ashes look good.'

They went by cab to the party. Archie Tindall was already there and Gina and Sam made a fuss of him. Archie enjoyed the attention and Gina thought she saw Hugo smiling from across the room.

During the evening, she obtained several drinks while her husband watched. Some she drank, others she abandoned or poured into the potted plants.

Later, when she had already feigned slight intoxication for Hugo's benefit, she flirted with Roger. As always, she felt a hint of danger in his presence.

'Your *décolletage* is entrancing this evening,' he said, glancing into her cleavage.

'How nice of you to notice.'

'It's impossible not to, dear Gina.'

'Surely you are not suggesting I am being obvious?'

'Never obvious. Simply voluptuous.' He glanced down at her breasts again. 'Ah, I remember them well.' He raised his eyes to hers and smiled. 'You get better with age.'

'Thirty is not age, Roger. I can still pretend to be twenty nine.' Her smile became taunting. 'Now forty is age.'

'Cruel girl. But I suppose you are right. The only good thing about me getting older is that I really am getting better with age.'

'You are?'

'Hard to believe, I know.' He smiled as if they were sharing a secret. 'As I recall, you never had cause to complain about my . . . stamina?'

'I take it you are not talking about the London Marathon?'

'Very droll. I'm talking about sex.'

'What a surprise.'

His smile became a grin.

'These days I can last forever.'

'You're obviously going out with the wrong girls.'

His lips curled in a smirk. Even smirking, Roger was good-looking.

'That sounds like a challenge.'

'Roger! The very idea. I'm a married woman.'

His voice dropped and the smirk became intimate.

'You're still the most exciting woman I've ever made love to, Gina. I don't suppose there is any chance of a reprise? It is my birthday.'

Gina knew his offer was serious.

'From what you say, we would need a whole weekend away before you . . .'

She left the sentence unfinished.

'Before I came?'

Now he was challenging her.

'Yes. Before you came.'

'Not with you. With you I could always come. Any time, anywhere. Remember?'

Gina smiled. She remembered. The memory was making her stomach flutter. She had made him come in a box at Covent Garden, on the Tube and on the back seat of a London bus. Roger had always had a penchant for sex in unusual places.

'I remember,' she said.

He stroked her cheek with a finger that trailed onto her neck. Gina was aware that her husband was watching.

'The bus?' he said. 'I thought I was going to choke you.'

'The conductor thought you were epileptic.'

'For about ten seconds I was.'

'All in the past, Roger.'

When he spoke again, his voice was low and even more dangerous.

'You could still make me come quickly. Five minutes, no more.' The tip of his finger lay lightly beneath her chin. He moistened his lips. 'With your hands. In your mouth. Inside you?'

Gina bent her head and kissed the finger.

'Dreams of the past,' she said. 'They are best left there.' Except when Hugo wanted her to recount them. He was still watching. She could feel his gaze from across the room. 'Besides, I love my husband.'

'Good God, Gina. I'm not suggesting you run away and leave your husband.' He chuckled. 'I'm suggesting a quick fuck for old time's sake.'

His roguish smile and their shared past allowed him to say such a thing and Gina smiled. Saying it had also been calculated. It was meant to add fire to the content of their conversation and it did.

'You put it so well.'

'I always did, didn't I?'

She laughed.

'You're incorrigible. Go fuck your girlfriend.'

'I will, later. But I'm offering you my virginity.'

'Virginity?'

'My first fuck since reaching forty.'

'My husband is watching us.'

'I know.'

Roger looked across the room and caught Hugo's eye. He put an arm around her shoulders and turned her towards Hugo and pointed in his direction. Gina laughed and waved and Roger toasted him with the drink he held.

Gina said, 'If you'll excuse me, I'll go and join him.'

'Of course.' As an afterthought, he said, 'I wonder – can he lip-read?'

Hugo was alone. She leaned her body against him and kissed his cheek. He put his hand around her waist and let it slip over her hip. His fingers traced a strap of the garter belt.

'Bored?' she asked.

'On the contrary. It's a nice party.'

'I suppose so.' She half turned so that her hip brushed against his groin. 'But predictable.'

'How so?'

'Roger. He propositioned me. Whenever I see him, he always propositions me.'

'You used to have a thing going with him, didn't you?'

'A long time ago.'

'Do you still find him attractive?'

'He's attractive.' She turned and kissed Hugo on the cheek. 'Not as attractive as you. But more attractive than Archie Tindall.'

Gina leaned her back against her husband so she could watch the activity in the room. She could feel his erection against her buttocks.

'Attractive enough to accept his proposition?' he said.

She leaned her head back against his shoulder.

'I don't love him. I love you.'

'What was his proposition? To love him?'

'No.' She licked her lips. 'To fuck him.'

It was as if an electric charge had been applied to her husband. His penis, already stiff, jumped against her.

Hugo's voice dropped an octave.

'Could you?' he said.

'Could I?' she said, making her voice sound as if it was affected by alcohol. 'Could I what?'

'Fuck him?'

She stared at Roger on the other side of the room and pretended to consider the proposition.

'I suppose so. If I wasn't married to you.'

'When you knew him before? Did you fuck him then?'

Hugo was coming out of the closet early this evening. Probably because he thought she was already at the point where her memory would lapse with the morning about what they had said and done. Conveniently lapse.

'Yes. I fucked him then.'

'Was he good?'

'He was quite good.'

Hugo's hands were on her hips, holding her steady. His penis pulsed between the cheeks of her bottom. She felt he might lose control and come here and now, in his trousers.

Gina finished the drink she held, hiccupped gently, and waved the empty glass.

'Need a refill,' she said. She stepped away from him with a discreet stagger. 'Last drink and then we'll go. If I'm not back in five minutes you'd better come looking for me.' She smiled sweetly and kissed him on the lips. 'I might need rescuing.'

The drinks were in another room and she weaved through the crowds of people towards the door knowing her husband was watching her. How far should she go with her flirtatious behaviour and intoxication? How long would it be before he wanted to go home and continue the game in private?

How far did she want to go?

Gina felt as if she were in a sexual free-fall. What happened was now in the hands of fate and Hugo. He could pluck her up any time he liked and take her back to the apartment for his sole pleasure.

It was up to Hugo to set the limits but she was still his tutor. She should ensure that they did not force the pace to a point where he might feel threatened. To a point where he might feel incapable of completing the course.

Chapter 13

A blues band played in the basement where couples danced. In a ground floor room at the front of the house, a young good-looking man with dark hair was playing a baby grand piano and singing Frank Sinatra songs.

Gina watched from the doorway as she sipped the full glass of wine. She felt Roger's presence behind her.

'He's good,' she said.

'I found him in a club in the Tottenham Court Road. Weddings, funerals and bar mitzvahs at reasonable prices.'

'You sound like his agent.'

'He doesn't need one. He's never short of bookings, or admirers.' Two young women were leaning over the piano watching him. 'It looks as if he's earned a bonus tonight.'

'Lucky young man.'

'What about my bonus?'

He moved closer against her so that his groin pushed against her buttocks.

'You don't deserve one.'

'My present?'

'We gave you port.'

'Much appreciated.' His hand moved over her hip. It found a strap of the garter belt. A finger traced it down to the stocking. 'But my virginity is still on offer.'

'You were always so generous, Roger.'

'Come on, Gina. You want it. I can tell.'

His erection began to grow against her. Simply by standing so close to her and talking about the possibility of sex had aroused him. Gina licked her lips. It had aroused her, too. Where was Hugo?

She turned to face Roger and continued to sip the wine.

'Almost time to go,' she said.

'You never used to be Cinderella.'

'Tonight I have a hot date.'

'With whom?'

'Hugo.'

'Hugo? A hot date?' His expression was quizzical. 'Bed socks, electric blanket and a good book?'

She laughed lightly.

'Something like that.'

'You still want it, Gina. I can see it in your face. You want it.'

'I'm going to get it.' She ran her tongue over her lips. 'When we get home, Hugo will fuck my brains out.'

The certainty of the words confused him. She smiled, a little drunkenly, and yawned behind her raised hand.

'Too much wine,' she said. 'We'd better leave while I'm still capable of enjoying it.'

'You're really leaving?'

'After a visit to the bathroom.' She looked over his shoulder and down the corridor. 'God, is there still a queue?'

'No matter how many bathrooms you have, there will always be a queue at any party with more than three women.'

'Sexist pig.'

'There are two more bathrooms upstairs. Shall I show you the way?'

'Can I trust you?'

'Of course not.'

'I'll find them.'

Gina put her glass into his hand and walked past him to the main staircase. Hugo should be watching, if he had any sense. In the likelihood that he was, she walked with the correct hint of unsteadiness.

In the bathroom, she looked at herself in the mirror. How dangerous was this particular game? She licked her lips. At the moment, she didn't care because she was enjoying it too much. Her stomach churned deliciously.

Roger was a predator. She was pretending to be tipsy for her husband's benefit, but Roger might also have been fooled and could be ready to take advantage. He might think she was ripe for seduction. Hugo might also think she was vulnerable to other men. What would he do about it? A variety of scenes and possibilities flashed through her mind.

If Hugo caught her in flagrante, would he hit Roger? Would he hit her?

Her husband, she felt, was far too much of a gentleman to strike a woman. But might he hit Roger? The thought of sudden pain and retribution being meted out to her former lover because she had allowed him to believe she was available for a lustful dalliance excited her even more.

God, what was she turning into? She abhorred violence. But, somehow, this seemed different. This was a game, wasn't it? Besides, nothing might happen. Roger might have been sidetracked downstairs, by his girlfriend or one of the many other desirable women attending the party. There was another possibility, one that made the hairs on the back of her neck stand on end as she considered it. Perhaps she really had had too much to drink because only now was she assessing what Hugo had said.

Could she fuck Roger?

Hugo had asked the question almost as if it was an invitation to go ahead and do so.

Is that what he wanted? Or was her ability to differentiate between fantasy and reality so impaired that she could no longer tell?

Her lips were dry again and she licked them once more. The wine, the evening, her underwear, her desire, all combined to confuse clear thought. There was no longer any point in trying to work out consequences. She was in the middle of a chain of events and must see where they led. Probably to her husband and home and sex.

Gina left the bathroom. Roger was waiting outside. There was no one else in the corridor. She had warned her husband to be ready to rescue her, hadn't she? Whatever happened would not be her fault.

'Are you really going?' Roger said.

'Yes.'

Her mouth was dry again. Did the need really show in her face?

He motioned to a room.

'I'll help you find your coat.'

Gina entered the room which held twin beds. Coats and wraps lay across them in disorganised piles like expensive jumble. The room was illuminated by a lamp on a bedside table. A dressing table was at the foot of the beds, on the opposite side of the room from the door.

She walked to the dressing table and looked in the mirror and flicked hair from her face. Roger was behind her. His arms came around her waist and he pulled her against him. His erection was already evident.

'No, Roger,' she said.

'Oh, yes, Gina.'

His hands moved. His right hand went over her breasts and into the front of her dress. It felt her flesh. The other went over her stomach and between her legs and rubbed at the juncture of her thighs. He bent his head and kissed her neck. In the mirror, through half-closed eyes, she saw Hugo in the doorway, hidden by the half-open door.

He was watching their reflection.

Gina turned, turning Roger with her so he would remain unaware of her husband's presence. Now his erection pressed against her stomach and he pulled her towards him for a kiss.

'No,' she murmured. She said it loud enough for her husband to hear.

She pretended to push Roger away with arms that were trapped within his embrace but put no power into her effort. He kissed her, covering her lips with his, forcing his tongue inside her mouth.

Gina felt herself responding. The twitch in her lower stomach refused to be denied. His erection rubbed against it and activated her little beast.

Their mouths broke apart and still she pretended to resist.

'Don't. No, don't.'

Over his shoulder, she caught a glimpse of Hugo still watching their reflection from the doorway.

Roger opened the front of the dress and pulled free her breasts. He buried his face in them while his hands tugged up her skirt and went beneath it. They crossed the nylon of the stockings and moved onto the flesh above. They gripped her buttocks and pulled her harder against him.

'No,' she murmured urgently. An urgency that might be interpreted two ways. 'No, you mustn't,' she said. 'Stop. Please stop.'

He kissed her again to silence her protests. When their mouths broke apart she lolled in his arms.

'Roger, I'm tired. I've had too much to drink. You mustn't do this.'

'You want it, Gina.' His fingers went between her legs and beneath the panties. They stroked apart the lips of her vagina and she gasped. 'I know you want it,' he said.

'No. Where's Hugo?'

Her voice had become distant, as if she were slipping into a dream.

Roger said, 'We'll find him in a minute. Don't worry.' His voice was cracking with tension. 'In a minute.'

She did not know how it happened but he turned her and applied pressure on her shoulders and she dropped to her knees between the beds. He knelt behind her.

'No,' she murmured again, as he pushed her forward over the bed. 'No, you mustn't. Only Hugo.'

'This is Hugo,' Roger said.

He lifted her skirts around her waist. His fingers were tugging down her panties. It should not have gone this far, surely? Hugo was there; he had heard her say no. He had heard her say only him. He could have stopped it at any time, he could stop it now. But he didn't.

Games.

Roger pulled her panties down around her thighs and his fingers went inside her. She was wet and he made her wetter. She was unable to suppress a groan. His finger reached from between her legs to stroke her clitoris and she reacted by pushing her bottom towards him.

'Hugo?' she said.

'Yes,' Roger said.

She heard him unzip his trousers and waited, her face lying against a fur wrap, smelling a hint of perfume from it, wondering how this situation had developed, unable to fully believe what was happening. That another man was about to enter her while her husband watched.

Had she miscalculated? Had the tuition got out of hand? Was she mistaken about the man in the doorway? Perhaps it was not her husband.

But nothing could stop Roger now and she did not want anything to stop him. She was highly aroused. What he had said before might not have been correct then, but it was now. She wanted it.

His hands opened her from behind and she felt him guide the tip of his penis towards her heat. He stroked it there, along the mouth of her vagina, as if kissing the lips. She gasped and moved backwards onto it, encouraging its entry. He tilted his hips and it went inside. It was a fluid entry because she was so wet.

He held her hips and his rhythm was instant and quick. She should have known he would want to do it in a room with the door open, a room into which anyone might walk at any time. He had always liked that edge of danger . . . and so had she. Did he know someone watched? Did he suspect it might be her husband?

Gina groaned, despite her reservations, and his fingers came around and dipped into her pubic valley and stroked her little beast.

'Not long,' he murmured behind her, his breath a rasp.

His finger rubbed and she sensed the change in his rhythm and the contractions and twitches of his penis and gave up pretence at control.

'Hugo,' she said, almost in despair, a last remnant of her pretence, and she buried her face into the fur and came.

Roger held her by the hips as she spasmed, his penis buried deep inside her and immobile and, as she finished, he heaved three, four times more, and grunted into his own orgasm.

The release had been marvellous and now she really was almost on the edge of a dream-state as she wallowed in the aftermath where tensions had become fluffy clouds upon which to float.

Gina felt a kiss on the neck and Roger withdrew from her. He pulled up her panties and pushed down her skirt and got to his feet. She listened to the rustle of his clothes as he re-fastened his trousers.

From the corridor outside, Hugo said, 'I'm looking for Gina.' He appeared to be talking to another guest. 'It's time we went.'

'In here, old boy,' Roger called moving to the dressing table and leaning back against it on his haunches.

Gina, still affected by the lethargy of completed sex, still on her knees, raised herself from the bed and looked round towards the door.

'Hugo?' she said.

Her husband stepped into the room. He smiled.

'There you are.' he said. 'Ready to go?'

'Yes.'

Had it been Hugo standing in the doorway watching? Had she made another miscalculation? How much had he seen? How much did he know or suspect?

122

Roger said, 'I was helping her find her coat.'

'That's very kind,' Hugo said, 'but we didn't bring any coats.'

Roger laughed.

'No wonder we couldn't find them.'

Gina got to her feet. She smiled tentatively and staggered a little. She really had had too much to drink.

'I think I've had too much to drink,' she said.

'I think you're right,' her husband said.

He said it with kindness and understanding and held an arm out towards her. She moved to him and leaned against his body and his arm went around her waist. He kissed her forehead.

'It's been an amusing party,' he said to Roger. 'But time we went.'

'Gina thought you might be bored.'

'Not at all. I'm never bored when I'm with Gina. Thanks again.'

'I should thank you. Both of you.' His smile broadened. 'For coming.'

Hugo continued to smile at Roger and Gina glanced at her former lover before they left the room. An accusing glance, but she knew it would cause him no regrets. Her husband held her hand as they walked along the corridor and down the stairs into the large circular reception hall.

'I called a cab,' he said. 'Should we say goodnight to Sam?'

'Yes. We must. Perhaps she wants to leave, as well.'

Hugo left her and walked a few yards down a corridor to the room that contained the bar. He waved an arm and Sam joined him. Gina saw them exchange words and then they both came towards her.

'Sam is staying,' Hugo said.

'I've not got a lot to go home to,' Sam said, with a feeble smile.

Gina wondered what she herself would be going home to.

Hugo kissed Sam's cheek and opened the double glass doors that led to the porch. The three of them were alone here, in an island of quiet. The noise of the party seemed to belong to a stage production of which they were part of the audience, escaping early.

Sam stared into Gina's eyes, her look concerned. Perhaps she could see something of the uncertainty she felt, Gina thought.

'Are you all right?' Sam said.

Gina smiled.

'I'm fine.'

Sam touched her hair, stroked it, to show her love, and Gina was aware of her husband standing close by, watching them both.

'I'll call you,' Sam said, and kissed her lightly on the lips.

Gina did not know what prompted her to do what she did, but she raised her hand to cradle Sam's head. Their lips parted briefly after that first, light kiss. Then Gina returned it with a kiss of passion instead of friendship.

She pushed her mouth against that of Sam who, initially, opened her eyes wide and pulled away in shock. But the cradle of Gina's hand held her head in place and, unbelievably, Sam no longer retreated. Her eyelids flickered and closed, her mouth responded and the kiss softened. Their lips parted and their tongues made gentle invasions of each other's mouths.

When they broke apart, they were both breathless and embarrassed. Gina had forgotten Hugo was there, standing two feet away, watching the kiss.

Sam still did not know how or why it had happened but to Gina it seemed inevitable after all that had preceded it. Yet as soon as she thought that, she regretted the reasoning, for it devalued her love for her friend.

Did everything have to be reduced to consequences as part of the game? Even her love for Sam? Had the kiss been delivered for the benefit of her husband? Or herself? The real consequence was unthinkable: the kiss had been wonderful. It had made her forget her husband was there.

'I'll call you,' she whispered to Sam, and turned and went past Hugo into the darkness.

Chapter 14

The evening had not gone as Gina had planned. It had gained its own momentum.

In the taxi on the way home, she lay her head on Hugo's shoulder and he placed a hand upon her thigh. Her head lolled, as if in sleep, and he slid his hand beneath her skirt and onto the flesh above her stockings.

Gina panicked momentarily, in case his hand went higher and found the wetness between her legs, but the journey did not take long. Her mind was lost in a confused debate with itself about how much he knew. About that final kiss with Sam. But once in the apartment, debate became redundant.

'Straight to bed,' he whispered.

His hands were insistent as he directed her.

In the bedroom, he stripped back the sheets with one hand before laying her on the mattress. She mumbled a protest about her clothes.

'You sleep, darling. I'll undress you.'

She had no option but to obey. He would find her wet between her legs and her panties stained. Would he know what with? Would he guess what had happened? Was he fired by his imagination or by what he had seen?

Gina rolled on the bed. Her bed, their bed. She knew its dimensions and its smell and its warmth. She felt comfortable on this bed; she felt safe. And she was tired. The recent past became distant. There was only now.

Perhaps he would not ask her for a story tonight. She had prepared one in her mind, rehearsed it to herself earlier in the day, but thought it was no longer suitable after what had transpired at the party with Roger. Perhaps tonight Hugo had no need for a story.

Her husband stripped naked. Through the tiredness, she was aware of him removing his clothes as he stood by the side of the bed, all the time staring at her. She was on the edge of sleep when she felt her skirt being raised. He had placed it about her waist but was not otherwise touching her.

Gina pushed away the tiredness. Her eyes remained closed but she sensed he was still standing by the bed, looking at her. What was he doing? Her tongue licked her lips as if in the midst of an arid dream, and she realised he was masturbating.

Her hips moved, slightly, before she could stop them, and he stopped his solitary act and knelt upon the bed beside her. He unbuttoned the front of the dress and unfastened the belt. His hands took a detour and went inside the cups of the brassiere to feel her breasts. The touch was gentle so as not to awaken her, so that she could remain asleep.

Hugo rolled her onto her stomach and pulled the dress from her shoulders and down her arms. He moved from the bed to tug it down her legs. She heard its soft rustle as he dropped it on the floor.

Again, he remained standing by the bed, looking at her

body in its provocative underwear. His breathing had changed. He still masturbated.

He got back onto the bed, and knelt behind her, his knees straddling her thighs, his erect penis laying between the cushions of her buttocks upon the silk of the flimsy panties. He unclipped the bra and pushed it from her shoulders. He leaned forward and kissed her back and his penis dug harder against her. His hips moved and it rubbed against the silk.

Hugo moved to one side and rolled her onto her back. He removed the bra and his mouth moved over her breasts. He suckled one then the other, flicking her nipples with his tongue, biting gently upon the flesh.

Now his hands tugged at her panties and she remembered what she had forgotten in the pleasures of the last ten minutes: the wet stickiness between her legs. His hands slid beneath her, to ease the silk over her buttocks. He tugged the sides from her hips until the silk lay like a thin strip at the apex of her legs.

They had stuck to her between her thighs and he moved them lower still, a few inches lower until they reached the tops of her stockings. His fingers fluttered over the soft skin of her inner thighs, pushing them apart, and moved inexorably upwards as if they knew what they were searching for.

Fingers slid onto the stickiness caused by another man's sperm. They spread it, massaged it, and took it on their tips when they moved higher to her still open vagina. The fingers slipped inside her and discovered the extent of her arousal and readiness. They stirred and probed and she groaned and her hips moved.

Her little beast needed to be touched and Hugo touched it. The fingers, now slick with sex, rubbed into the upper valley of her vagina and rolled her waiting clitoris.

Gina gasped, her head moved languorously on the pillow, and she stayed in the dream state between sleep and reality as her body was overcome with the sensations that emanated from her core, sensations that were enhanced by images of her husband scooping another man's seed upon his fingers to provoke her to orgasm.

If receiving this alien sperm had been a sin then he was absolving her of guilt with this beautiful anointment. He had been watching, she knew that now, and therefore the guilt was shared, even if she was asleep, even if this orgasm that grew with total inevitability was in her dreams, for that was still the way he wanted it, that was still the game.

Gina came, her thighs pressing together, her mouth opening, her breath gasping from her body. His fingers waited in place until her contractions had finished. Now she was very close to sleep and, as if he understood the tranquilising effect of her climax, his hands became more demanding.

He pulled the panties down her legs and off her feet and it was only then that she realised she still wore her high-heeled shoes. He spread her legs and knelt between them and she felt the heat of the tip of his penis as it rested against her open vagina.

But he paused and waited and she risked a glance from beneath her eyelashes to see why he delayed and saw that he held the stained and sticky panties to his face. His eyes were closed, perhaps reliving those few heated minutes in the dimly lit bedroom at the party, and his nostrils flared at the aromas the silk contained.

Gina closed her own eyes and moved her vagina to nudge his penis. He regained purpose and leaned over her. With one hand he held his erection and rubbed it slowly inside the lips of her sex. She was hot and wet and he stirred the mixed juices and prepared to add his own, but at his own pace, in his own way.

She rolled her head and spread her arms, a victim yet again, and he began his entry. His penis was hard and large and pulsing with an urgency he was attempting to restrain. But she consumed it in her heat and felt it begin to boil, felt him realise it was unsustainable.

His hips made the decision for him and he began to buck upon her, driving it deeply inside, attempting to drive it further than her lover's, scouring her of other men's lust and filling her with his own. He pulled her thighs up so that her high-heels dug into the bed. He gripped her hips and, all the time, he held himself above her and she felt his stare upon her face.

As he came, words escaped with the grunts from his throat.

'Fuck!' and 'Whore!'

But then he was lost in the fury of his orgasm and he shuddered and fell upon her and held her shoulders and kissed her neck and she thought she felt his tears upon her cheek.

Gina did not know how long he lay upon her for now she really did fall asleep.

Gina was awakened in the night by Hugo having sex with her from behind.

She lay on her side and her husband was spooned around her. His rhythm was steady and she guessed he had been maintaining it for some while. His penis moving inside her was a pleasant adjunct to her dreams and she did not let him know she had awakened.

They were covered by a sheet and she realised she no longer wore her shoes, although she did still wear the garter belt and stockings. The straps made her feel she was in bondage to sex, to be used at her husband's whim. It was another pleasant fancy to play with in the laziness of her mind.

She went back to sleep before he finished.

Dawn woke her early. The light bloomed through the uncurtained window. Gina slipped from the bed, leaving Hugo asleep, pulled the curtains closed to retain the illusion of night, and went to the bathroom.

She arched pleasurably from the sex and the insides of her thighs were slick with juices that had not had time to dry. She put on a shower cap and let hot water soothe and cleanse her and avoided thinking of what had occurred the night before.

That had been alcohol and the game. Today was guilt and uncertainty. There was also the kiss, but that was too embarrassing to consider. It was something about which to make an excuse.

Her reflection in the mirror did not impress her and she applied fresh make-up and brushed her hair. She added a discreet touch of perfume and returned to bed naked. Hugo slept on and she slipped in beside him but at a distance. She left the sheet at her waist so that her breasts were exposed and lay facing him and closed her eyes.

This time her sleep was shallow and her thoughts were daydreams that could be manipulated rather than the dreams of slumber that could not. She was aware when Hugo stirred. He grunted and changed his position, breathed in deeply once and exhaled even more deeply as if regretting that morning had arrived. She knew his routine of waking, but this morning he did not follow a routine. She felt him looking into her face.

For a long time, he did not move. Then the mattress creaked gently and she smelled his fingers before they touched her cheek. His fingers still had the smell of sex which, the morning after, had a delicious hint of degeneracy. What she and Hugo had done belonged to the shadows of the night. Flaunting the aroma of their couplings upon his fingers was acknowledging their behaviour.

His hand moved over her shoulder and down her arm. He touched her breasts, stroked her nipples. Her eyes remained closed, her breathing even.

Hugo pushed back the sheet and slid from the bed. Her breathing deepened in disappointment. She heard the shower and wondered if he had abandoned her to get ready for work. But perhaps he had seen she was clean and fresh and had decided to follow her example?

She looked at the imprint of his head on the pillows. A small piece of blue silk peeped from beneath them. She reached and found her panties. Delicately, she lifted them to her nose and inhaled a cocktail of smells that were genuinely intoxicating. Her other hand went between her legs and touched herself.

Memories, guilt, the need to expiate her indiscretion, the desire to fuck her husband, made her so sensitive that she groaned at her own touch. She rubbed herself with a desperate need and her little beast responded, demanded, shrieked silently for more, and she came, so swiftly her mouth opened in surprise as she rocked upon her fingers.

The shower stopped and she pushed the panties back

beneath Hugo's pillow and rolled onto her side so that he would not see the flush in her face if he returned.

Please make him return!

He returned and slid back into bed. His body was cool from walking naked in the apartment. He pushed it against her from behind. Cool everywhere but at his groin where his penis was erect and hot.

Hugo kissed her neck and his hand stroked her body. His knee pushed between her legs from behind and he slid his penis between her thighs. His palm caressed a breast. His tongue slid along her neck to her ear and dipped wetly inside. She moaned and moved against him.

'Awake?' he whispered.

'Yes.'

'I love you.'

'I love you, too.'

'Always and completely. I didn't know how much until . . .' He kissed her neck again. 'Always and completely.'

'Good.'

She snuggled against him, moving the softness of her buttocks against his groin.

'Last night,' he said, hesitantly. He was still testing the new ground of morning, even though they lay in the shadows behind drawn curtains. 'Last night when I saw you with Roger.'

Gina held her breath. How far was he going?

'You looked a couple. Do you know what I mean? You looked good together.'

He was still staying within the parameters of the game. She was relieved.

'We were a couple, for a time.'

'I know. I just hadn't thought about it before. Were you good together?'

'Good together?'

If he wanted to know, he had to say it. Had to ask. This was also part of the game. She had made it easier for him by laying with her back to him so he did not have to look into her face.

'Sexually. Was the sex good?'

'Yes. It was good.'

He kissed her neck again.

'Was he a good fuck?' he whispered.

'Yes,' she whispered back. 'He was a very good fuck.'

Hugo's penis twitched between her thighs.

'Tell me about him,' he said. 'Tell me what you did. Tell me how you fucked him.'

Her husband was making progress. He no longer needed the cover of her insobriety or the night. He was now asking questions in the dawn.

'He fucked me everywhere.'

'Everywhere?'

He was confused.

'Roger liked fucking in unusual places. He liked the possibility of being found out, of being watched. He enjoyed it if he knew someone else was there.'

'Did you fuck him while someone watched?'

'Yes.'

Hugo's breathing changed.

'Did you know they were watching?'

'Yes.'

'Another man?'

'Yes.'

Her husband licked his lips before he kissed her ear.

'Did the other man do anything?'

'He wanted to. Roger wanted him to. Roger wanted him to fuck me as well.'

'Did he? Did he fuck you? Did you let the other man fuck you?'

He wanted her to say yes.

'Yes,' whispered Gina. 'They both fucked me.'

Hugo licked her neck and his hand caressed her breast. His penis twitched against her vagina.

'Tell me,' he said. 'Tell me what happened.'

Chapter 15

'It happened at a wedding,' Gina said. 'When Sam and Brian got married six years ago. Roger and I had been seeing each other for three or four months. It had been an intense affair. He was very highly sexed, as if he had to prove his masculinity by doing it often.'

'Doing it?' prompted Hugo.

'Fucking,' she said.

He moved his penis between her legs. The insides of her thighs were becoming moist with its secretions.

'Go on,' he said.

'There were about a hundred guests. The wedding was at a small church in Sussex. The reception at a country hotel. It happened at the hotel.'

He continued kissing her neck and moving against her, but his right hand now moved downwards, over her stomach, and his fingers pushed through her pubic hair. Her abdomen twitched as the fingers closed on their destination. He found her clitoris and began to move it gently beneath his fingertips.

'The reception was held in a function room with its own bar. On the other side of the hotel was a small cocktail bar that was closed. The grilles were down on the bar and it was in darkness. Roger took me there.'

'What were you wearing?'

'A silk suit. it was pale blue.

'What were you wearing underneath?'

'White underwear.'

'Stockings?'

'White stockings. Roger insisted I always wore stockings. And pale blue high heels.'

Almost every present Roger had bought her had been underwear and occasionally a dress for which he could see sexual potential. He had been candid about his generosity. Your present is my present, he would say, meaning he only bought items for Gina from which he would derive pleasure.

At the time, she had not complained. Invariably, the pleasure was mutual.

'We had been drinking champagne. Perhaps I had had too much. But when he took me away from the reception and into the cocktail bar, I knew his intentions.'

'Did you want to go?'

'Oh yes. I knew he would have something planned. I knew it would be exciting.'

'Go on.'

'The cocktail bar was in shadows. The carpet was dark red and the walls were wood-panelled. Dark wood. There were club chairs and a leather chesterfield. The chesterfield was maroon. The door didn't lock but that didn't bother Roger. To him, that was an advantage.

'He kissed me. His hands went over me. He groped me and pulled up my skirt until it was bunched around my waist. I kept looking over his shoulder in case someone came in. I wanted him to hurry up and get it over with but he didn't want that. He wanted to take his time.'

Roger had been excited and his excitement had been contagious. The fear of discovery had given an added edge to her arousal.

'What did he do?'

'He took me to the chesterfield and laid me upon it. My skirt was still around my waist. He knelt on the carpet and opened the top of the suit and pulled my breasts from the cups of my bra. He sucked my breasts while his hands touched me between my legs.'

'How did he touch you between your legs?'

'He pulled down my panties, pulled them all the way down and took them off and put them in his pocket. He opened my legs and touched my vagina. He opened it and pushed fingers inside me. He made me wet.'

'Did you like it? Did you like his fingers inside you?'

'Yes. Oh yes.'

'Then what did he do?'

'He kissed my thighs. My legs at the top of the stockings. He licked from the nylon onto the flesh. He licked alongside the straps up my thighs. He opened my legs wider and put his face between them. He licked my vagina. He licked my clitoris.' She momentarily pressed the fingers that were rolling the little bud right now. 'Yes, there. He kissed there. He covered my vagina with his mouth and he sucked and licked.'

Talking about it, remembering an event from the past she had buried beneath other memories, aroused Gina. She replaced the pressure on the fingers that rolled her clitoris and held them there.

Hugo whispered breathlessly in her ear.

'He sucked you?'

'Yes.'

'He licked you?'

'Yes.'

'Did it feel good?'

'It felt marvellous.'

'What happened?'

'I came.'

Gina, eyes closed, wrapped in her husband's lust, came upon his fingers and did not attempt to hide the intensity of the orgasm.

He kissed her as she recovered.

'Was that good?' he said.

'That was very good.'

His erection pounded between her wet thighs.

'Roger sucked you until you came?'

'Yes.'

'Did he do that often?'

'All the time.'

He eased himself away from her and rolled her onto her back. He did not look at her, but sucked her breasts while his fingers slid between the lips of her open sex.

'Tell me how he did it?' he whispered, his head sliding lower across her stomach.

'He opened my legs a little. Yes, like that. He kissed my stomach.' She guided his head with her hands, his tongue trailing over her skin, willing to go where it was directed. 'There,' she said, 'he licked there. Down there at both sides.'

He licked the creases of flesh where her thighs joined her torso, trailing two side of the triangle of her pubic hair.

'That's it,' she whispered, opening her legs a little more,

directing his head, feeling his breath upon her vagina. 'He kissed me there. Just there.'

His mouth covered her sex mouth and she held his head gently in place. He licked. His tongue delved. He sucked. He rubbed his face in her sex and fought his way to her clitoris. His mouth enveloped it and she moaned. She removed her hands from his head and let them lie by her side.

Hugo had discovered a new joy. He lapped and sucked without instruction and she let him. She wallowed in his attention and allowed another orgasm to build.

His hands went beneath her and held her bottom. He held her in both hands and ate her vagina. He grunted almost in delirium and she entered into a series of gasps that had only one conclusion. She pushed harder against his mouth and her thighs held his head in place and she came once more.

He seemed reluctant to trail his face back up her body but she pulled at his shoulders and he relinquished her vagina. He lay against her and kissed her neck. She reached for his penis and held it in a soft grip. She rubbed her face against his, smelling herself, licking her taste from his lips, as he kissed her.

When their mouths slid apart, she whispered, 'Shall I go on?' wanting to go on, wanting to excite him, to reward him, to tempt him further.

'Yes. Go on.'

He lay upon her and his penis was pushing at her sex. She reached between them and guided its head inside. His hips sank upon her, his penis pushing for depth. When it was totally immersed, he held it there without rhythm.

'Go on,' he whispered. 'What happened next?'

'Roger sucked me and I came. But he didn't stop. He kept sucking me, and I could feel another orgasm and was not far away and I didn't want him to stop. And then, over his shoulder, I saw the door to the bar open and another man came in. He was a business friend of Roger's. I had only met him briefly that day, didn't know him very well. Not then.'

Hugo moved tentatively inside her.

'What did he do?'

'Nothing, at first. He stood by the bar and watched. I lay upon the chesterfield with my skirt around my waist and my top open and my breasts spilling out. Roger continued to suck me and although I was shocked I was also excited.

'I pushed on Roger's shoulders to let him know someone was there but he ignored me. He never did admit it, but I think he arranged for the other man to join us. Told him to follow us into the bar after a certain time to be part of his show.'

Hugo had begun to reluctantly move his penis, as if he thought he might come too quickly if the friction was too strong. He rotated his hips so that he stirred her insides. She did the same in a slow screwing motion. It was obvious they both found it extremely satisfying.

Hugo said, 'Did he just watch?'

'He unfastened his trousers and took out his prick,' Gina said. 'As he watched, he masturbated.'

Her husband shuddered.

'What did you do?'

'I came again. I couldn't help it. Roger's mouth wouldn't stop and it was exciting. Watching a stranger masturbate.'

'Then what happened? After you came?'

'Roger had unfastened his trousers while he was kneeling

on the floor. As I recovered, he got on the chesterfield between my legs and put his prick inside me. I was too dazed to stop him. I still didn't understand why he hadn't noticed the other man. But it seemed as if he hadn't because he began fucking me.'

Hugo changed his movement and began to withdraw a little way before pushing it deep inside her again.

'How did he fuck you?'

'Hard. He fucked me hard.'

'Like this?'

He changed his strokes and pounded into her fiercely, holding her hips as he strained above her, withdrawing almost all the way before thrusting it back inside.

'Yes!' Gina's voice trembled because of the onslaught. 'Like this.' She groaned. 'No. It was not as good as this.'

Hugo continued with his assault a while longer before stopping. His penis lay embedded and at rest. He rested on his arms above her and they both gasped for breath. Sweat was on his forehead and she could feel her own perspiration beneath her breasts.

'That was good,' she murmured.

He lowered himself upon her, but kept his weight on his elbows and knees. He kissed her neck and ear.

'Go on,' he said. 'What happened next?'

'Roger stopped and lay upon me and I whispered to him that someone was watching. He looked over his shoulder and when he turned back he was grinning. It was as if he had fucked me hard as part of the show.

'He knelt up and told me to roll over but I wouldn't. I was nervous. He turned me over, pulling at my hips. I didn't want to but he had already done so much with an audience that I did not see how I could stop him continuing.

He turned me over so that I lay on my stomach. He pulled my hips up and knelt behind me. He pushed his prick in from behind. This time he fucked me slowly.'

Hugo fucked her slowly.

'And the other man?'

'He was still there. Standing by the grille at the bar. I turned my head away so I didn't have to watch. But he was still there, masturbating. He was smiling.'

'What was he like? This other man?'

'He was about the same height and age as Roger. They were older than me. I was twenty four, Roger is ten years older than me. The other man was heavier than Roger. I remember he had a thick neck because it bulged over his collar. He had dark hair but basically, he was nondescript.'

'Was he good-looking?'

'Neither good-looking nor ugly. I hadn't noticed him properly until he came into the cocktail bar and began to watch us. But he had cruel eyes and a neck that bulged over his collar.'

'Cruel eyes?'

'Yes.'

'Did he make you do things?'

'They both did.'

'What did they do?'

'They fucked me.'

Hugo groaned.

'Tell me.'

'Roger turned me onto my back again. The other man had moved closer. He was standing by the chesterfield. His hand was still moving on his prick. Roger kissed me. It was a sort of reassurance, to tell me everything was all right. That he was in control. I was in such a confused state, I didn't know how to behave. How to react. I could hardly scream for help when I had gone into a deserted bar for sex and hadn't complained when the other man walked in. I felt trapped.'

'What did you do?'

'Nothing. I just let things happen. I let them do what they wanted to do. I knew it would be over quickly. It had to be over quickly. I knew that would be the easiest way out.'

'What did they do?'

'Roger manoeuvred me on the chesterfield. There's no other way of describing it. He lay against the back of it and he pulled me so that I lay against him, facing him. He still kissed me. No words were said, but I knew from his eyes what was going to happen.

'He held me and kissed me. His prick lay against my stomach. I felt the other man get on the chesterfield behind me. His hands touched my bottom and I shuddered and Roger kissed me again, as if to soothe me, calm me down. His eyes said everything was all right. I remember staring into his eyes as the man behind me opened my legs and pushed his prick in me from behind.

'It was big and he pushed it straight in and I groaned when it went in. Not a groan of pleasure, more of disbelief. The man held my bottom, gripped the flesh and pushed it against himself, pushing it around his prick. Then he fucked me. Hard but taking his time. As if they had planned it. And all the time, Roger stared into my eyes, watching my reaction.

'He kissed me, as if to say good girl. And then he moved from beneath me, pulled himself upwards until his cock pushed against my breasts, until my face was in his lap and he pushed my head down and I took him in my mouth and sucked him.'

Her husband moaned and his body language changed. Instead of fucking her, he was now making love to her. She stroked the back of his head and kissed his neck.

'Shall I tell you the rest?'

'Yes.' It seemed he could hardly speak. 'Tell me.'

'After a while, they changed positions. The other man sat on the chesterfield and I knelt between his legs and sucked his prick. Roger knelt behind me and fucked me from behind. While he fucked me, he leaned over so that he could watch me suck. He kissed my cheek as I sucked.'

The words and images she was creating were obscene but they were filling her husband with turmoil and desire, and she was feeding from both her own lasciviousness and his lust. Gina felt as if she had shed restrictions, as if there were no limits to what she could imagine, the images she could create.

They filled her and Hugo with sex, they turned their bodies into total instruments of sex. Beyond sex there was nothing, beyond this coupling there was nothing. Their nerve ends were alive with sex that emanated physically and emotionally in waves that had totally enflamed them.

'Did they come?' Hugo said hoarsely.

'The man came in my mouth. Roger leaned round to watch as closely as he could. His face was only inches away. As the man came, Roger pulled my mouth away and the sperm splashed into my face. The sight made Roger come as well. He came inside me, his fingers rubbing at my clitoris as he came.'

'And you?' Hugo said. 'What about you?'

'I came. I couldn't help it. I came with sperm in my face and my head in a stranger's lap. I came with Roger fucking me from behind. I came.'

Hugo groaned and began to move upon her with purpose and she knew the time for talking was gone. At first, he was hesitant in his rage and his power, not sure whether he should be displaying lust or love, but Gina's aggression told him this was not a time to hold back.

Their love-making became a torrid contest in which their heaving bodies made demands upon each other, their mouths slid over each other's faces and their hands gripped flesh. Their sweat mingled with the juices of sex and saliva. He turned her on the bed and attacked her from different angles. She fought back and challenged him with her hips.

Her throat threatened to swallow his penis and had him gasping. Her finger, that probed through the sweat of his buttocks and gained entry into his anus, made him yell out, at first in surprise and then in pleasure.

They fucked and loved and the world for them could have ended and they would not have noticed, for their own world of self-generating sex was coming close to its own ending. Gina knew better than to expect simultaneous climaxes and when hers approached she accepted it and did not attempt to postpone it. She allowed herself to be swept up on its breaking waves and cried out as it took her and she shook beneath her husband.

Hugo paused, as if shipwrecked on her tremors, before plunging into her again, kneeling upon the bed and pulling her hips clear of the mattress and around his waist. Her body lay back and flipped about at his onslaught and she twisted and gasped because he had caught the end of the climax and it had refused to die.

A second orgasm grew within her and she slipped over the edge again as he came.

They lay together on the bed, limbs entwined. As her

body became cold with the drying sweat, Hugo moved from her to retrieve the covers from the floor. They lay together, cuddled and warm, and she went to sleep.

There was much to consider, but not now. Right now she ached pleasurably and was still dazed at the heights of sexual release they had reached. All this in a few weeks with the aid of her stories and a journal of indiscreet dialogue.

Was the journal now redundant? Or would it be used to prompt more adventures? Now Hugo had had a taste of what was there to be unleashed, who knew what he might desire?

Chapter 16

The day passed in an ordered fashion which seemed inappropriate, considering all that had happened.

Hugo brought Gina coffee in bed before he left to walk to his clinic in Harley Street. He kissed her forehead and said he wouldn't be late and after he'd gone she lay and wondered if anything would ever be the same again. When it was, she was both disappointed and relieved.

Gina wondered if she should call Sam as she had promised but didn't. Sam had also said she would call her. But Sam didn't.

Were they both embarrassed? Gina reasoned that the sooner she picked up the telephone and called her friend the sooner the embarrassment would be over and they could return to a normal relationship. Still she prevaricated. She didn't make the call.

Hugo returned home at six and her doubts and recriminations were once more submerged by normality. They dined and watched television and had an early night. He seemed so determined to be normal that his behaviour appeared almost formal. When they went to bed, he lay on his back and made no attempt to touch her, except to squeeze her hand and say goodnight. They slept.

The next morning he woke her with coffee and the morning newspapers. He was dressed and ready to leave for the clinic and she was surprised to see it was already ten thirty. After he had gone, the newspapers lost their interest.

How long had he been up? Had he continued their discreet dialogue in the journal? Was it waiting to be read?

She walked to the study naked. The journal was on the desk and there was a new entry. She sat at the desk and began to read.

It is as if I have wandered into a mansion of delights and each door I open presents yet another delectation. My regret is that I have wasted so many years before discovering this mansion which has so many doors and so many floors still to be investigated.

Yet I continue to feel the constraints of upbringing which has sapped my judgement. I would willingly leap into the deep end of experience and sink or swim but dare not for fear I might lose that which I hold most dear: the love of my wife.

For it is Gina who has led me so far, who has coaxed and coached me from my previously dormant state. I do not pretend to be skilled in the sexual arts but I am learning and a willing apprentice.

Before Gina eased me loose from that dreary routine of career and social commitments, I can honestly say that sex was rarely in my mind. Now it is a permanent beam, a light someone has left on, a switch that has been thrown in my circuitry which allows the power to flow without restraint every waking moment of the day and night and, often, in my dreams.

Previously, my sexual urges had atrophied. I had

placed a Do Not Disturb sign upon them. Because they were not used I had forgotten them. I did not read sexual magazines or literature. There were no stimulants in my life to urge me to indulge in such publications. I had no great erotic memories of the past to try to recreate in masturbation or to prompt me into renewed practice.

There were two girls with whom I made love, if it can be called that. I lost my virginity to a girl at university. I was drunk and grateful to have lost what I believed to be an encumbrance for a young man of my age. Once initiated into the mystery of putting a piece of my anatomy into a piece of hers, I did not feel the urge to repeat the exercise except as a way of proving my manhood.

This was an affair of little pleasure, mainly conducted at the young woman's instigation and whilst I was under the influence of drink.

It sounds scandalous, even to me, that this situation was allowed to happen and continue. I associated sex with narrow beds and dark rooms that smelled of cannabis and alcohol. I preferred the company of men, and enjoyed physical release through sport.

After leaving university I became aware of rumours, among the circle of acquaintances I had, about my sexual preferences because I did not have a regular female companion. I was still at an impressionable age and rectified the rumours, in my mind, by embarking on a brief and unsatisfactory affair with a young woman.

She was a pleasant enough young lady but, like me, of extremely limited experience and my interest was only to once more prove my manhood. All the relationship did was to fill me with guilt.

If I had loved her and been a more accomplished lover, I am sure she would have responded. But I did not and was not. She allowed me to lie upon her and we performed a mechanical act that produced, at least for me, the required climax. Our affair was not formally ended but simply died of its own accord.

Subsequently I put sex from my mind and concentrated on other things. My career was successful and I built a façade which rumours could not penetrate.

What did I care what others believed? Sex, I told myself, was a bestial pastime. Dogs did it in the street, so where was its place in the grand scheme of civilisation? It might be essential for propagation, but I was quite content not to be a propagator.

(I promised at the beginning of this journal small confessions. This seems to be bigger than the others).

It really is possible not to even think about sex in daily life, if daily life does not contain the stimulants of sex. Mine did not. I avoided books, theatre, films or television that might be frivolous, scurrilous or sensational. I preferred debates on a higher plain, serious books and music and cerebral pastimes.

Then I met Gina.

There had been other women. I had escorted ladies to social events and formed what I had thought were friendships. In retrospect, these were merely acquaintanceships that they, perhaps, had been expecting, hoping possibly, to develop. When they had not developed, they had no doubt wondered about my sexuality.

On occasions, these ladies had been quite beautiful but I had conditioned myself to consider beauty aesthetically, to appreciate them as I might a painting. Any twinges of desire I might have had were subdued by the memory of my past failings.

This was not a conscious act. I did not socialise whilst carrying a permanent fear of sexual disaster at the forefront of my mind. But because I could not countenance the embarrassment of failing again, I removed even the possibility of attempting a sexual liaison from my brain.

Instead, I preferred the façade of being a private man who was slightly mysterious and whose inclinations might even be termed asexual.

Then I met Gina.

I fell in love and even my past could not stop me wanting to be with her, wanting to marry her. My greatest fear was that I might lose her. Even this was surpassed and made me forget about our possible sexual incompatibility. I was overcome with happiness when she agreed to be my wife. Only then did I realise I would have to face my past and my sexual failings.

My hope was that together we would learn and develop, but then I realised she was much more experienced than I. This knowledge tormented me but was also a fascination. It made my love burn stronger. But how could I compete with all the men she had previously known?

Our love-making was, I know, a stilted affair. My desire was so great that I found it difficult to sustain an erection. To combat premature ejaculation, I took to masturbating in the bathroom before going to bed to enhance my durability.

(A minor confession now, set alongside all the others).

But still I was useless and felt the guilt of not being able to properly satisfy my beautiful wife.

Rather than attempt to extend my knowledge, I became rooted in what I knew: the mechanics of insertion and ejaculation. Until, at last, Gina showed me a way forward.

This journal has complemented her tuition and, in the process of learning and of expanding knowledge, has become something more.

The memories she shares of her past experiences burn my soul. What happened at the party two nights ago almost engulfed me.

I watched her with a former lover. Watched their flirtatious behaviour. Saw how the memories of what they had once shared still sparked her eyes, still made him wet his lips with want. I even prompted her, provoked her, with questions about the past, and I let her leave my presence even though I knew she was vulnerable and in need of protection.

When she went upstairs I saw him follow. I followed too, at a distance, out of sight. They entered a bedroom and I approached silently. Why silently? Even now I shake in my anguish at my motives. I approached silently hoping, and yet not hoping, to find them in an embrace, to watch them engaging in sexual exchanges. Hoping, and yet not hoping, to be a witness to Gina's past by watching her re-live it.

They were in an embrace and I remained a phantom, standing behind the partially opened door and watching what transpired in a mirror. The mirror put false distance between us. I told myself it was a window into the past. I knew I was lying to myself, making excuses for my inactivity.

He was molesting my wife. The sort of molestation that can be excused at parties because of high spirits and alcohol, because of aroused hopes and miscalculations. She tried to stop him. She said no, but he could have interpreted that as a salve to her conscience because, after all, she had gone into the room with him.

I did nothing. I did not intervene. I watched with a detachment that was belied by the fervour that boiled inside. He threw her over a bed and pulled up her skirts. He pulled down her underwear and knelt behind her. He pushed himself inside her and fucked her. He fucked her and I watched. Immobile. Frozen. On fire. He fucked her.

My emotions were a typhoon waiting for release.

He fucked her.

I watched.

Guilt, jealousy, love, desire, anger.

This is the nectar of the gods. A cup that has to be sipped to be understood and yet I still do not understand. I was consumed. I was beyond orgasm. This was a fusion of cerebral and emotional sex. The physical was yet to be indulged. This was immensity.

I was still in a daze when we left the party. Still playing the phantom. Still high on the ecstacy of the guilt. When Gina kissed Sam it was as if I had imbued them with my feelings, as if I had charged the very atmosphere.

They kissed. Mouths open, tongues licking. This was not an act. They kissed with wanton enjoyment as if I were not there.

When we got home, I was at last able to indulge the physical. The sex was sating, I thought, until I woke up and was inspired by my beautiful wife to begin again. She talked and she taught and I worshipped at her sex and buried my face between her legs and drank again of nectar.

How could I ever have doubted that I would be less than ecstatic about being allowed to sup at such a chalice?

My love is making my words cumbersome when what I want to say is fuck and suck. But both descriptions have their place, both are valid, for romance and sex intermingle effortlessly if they are allowed their way.

So far, all this has been by way of a confession. Now I shall record what Gina and I did when we returned from the party, and re-tell her account of the occasion when she was taken by two men at the same time.

Hugo went into great detail in both instances. His language became less poetic, his descriptions objective rather than subjective. 'Fuck' and 'suck' became prominent. His handwriting became large and shaky.

Gina had been part of what was being described but felt like a stranger. This was a different version to be the one she had experienced. Her story had metamorphosised into rape. But his narrative was effective and by the time she had reached the end her emotions were as ragged as his handwriting.

As before, he had left a space to indicate a break and when he had resumed his entry, his writing had become steady once again and his statements reasoned and considered. But now she read with a butterfly of fright in her stomach.

Whereas before, my mind automatically refused to acknowledge anything of a sexual nature, now it is open to all influences. I stare at young women in the street and wonder about their underwear and how they look when they are being fucked. Every newspaper is full of innuendo, every magazine stand a cornucopia of promise. Now my mind is open, it attracts and is attracted by anything sexual. I am permanently attuned to sex.

I have read widely in the last few weeks in an attempt to understand the deluge of feelings I have unleashed in myself and to understand more fully the needs and desires of my wife, and I have discovered that women fantasise even more than men.

My own fantasy was fulfilled the other night when I watched another man have sex with Gina, and yet it was an incomplete fantasy, a cerebral and emotional experience that lacked physical involvement.

Does one fantasy inevitably lead to another? Is there ever fulfilment?

I have read that the single greatest fantasy of women is to be dominated and forced to perform sex. To be guiltlessly taken again and again. To be released from responsibility. To be forced to do the unthinkable. To be forced to do what they want to do.

Of course, this is fantasy. The women who dream of such perverse delights are always safe, there is no pain, no real compulsion, and the men in their fantasy who perpetrate the abuse can be ciphers or handsome lovers or German Shepherd dogs or any deviant they wish to create.

My fantasy is to release my beautiful wife from responsibility and make the fantasy real. This would be imagination brought to life, with no recriminations, no questions and no guilt. There need never be acknowledgement that it ever even happened for it is fantasy, after all.

A dream of intense erotic pleasure that, for once, comes true.

Could this happen? I think so, with care. With safeguards and, perhaps, building to it in stages, leaving escape doors along the way. A fantasy in stages. The first one simple. Sharing my wife with another man.

But paramount in any plan has to be the tacit approval of my wife. I have to ensure that anything that happens would not be abhorrent or oppressive. Gina cannot be coerced or bullied, she must enter willingly into those other rooms in that mansion of delight. For my first duty is to protect the love of my wife.

Gina sat for a long time staring at the final few paragraphs her husband had written in the journal. She did not re-read them. She did not have to.

At last, she got up and went into the bedroom. She found her address book, looked up the telephone number and called Sam.

'I need to see you,' she said.

Chapter 17

They met at Sam's apartment in St Katherine's Dock near the Tower of London. It had a view over the marina and the Thames. Gina had stressed an Italian restaurant was not the place to discuss the latest chapter of the journal.

Gina stood by the picture window, sipped a large gin and tonic and stared out. The view was spectacular but she did not appreciate it. She waited while Sam, who sat on the large oatmeal couch, read the photocopied pages she had brought.

Neither had mentioned the kiss. The urgency of Gina's request had relegated it to be considered at another time. Perhaps a long time in the future when it could be referred to as an amusing incident that had been staged for Hugo's benefit. Perhaps.

Except that Hugo referred to the kiss in the journal. Gina had considered removing the reference in the photocopies but had felt that would have been dishonest. Besides, this was a way of having it accepted without the need to speak of it. There was enough debate in the rest of the pages.

Sam was taking a long time. Gina glanced at her, but her head was down and she only seemed half way through the photostats.

'You're taking a long time,' Gina said.

'There's a lot to take in.'

Gina finished the drink and poured herself another. Ice tinkled in her glass.

'Does yours want freshening?' she asked.

Without looking up, Sam handed the glass to her. It was empty. Gina poured her another and added ice and lemon. She placed it back in Sam's hand.

'Thanks,' Sam said, without looking up.

Gina went back to the window but still did not appreciate the view. She turned her back to it and watched Sam.

Sam had suggested coming here without hesitation when she heard the urgency in Gina's voice. Gina hoped she hadn't sounded too urgent. After all, they were only meeting to discuss pages from a journal, not to organise the farewell orgy on the Titanic.

Two nights ago, the evening had gained its own momentum and she had become carried in its wake. She had thought she would be able to recover control but it now seemed as if the sexual awakening of her husband had gained the upper hand. That the fire they had created together had blazed beyond control.

He had suggested in the journal that if sexuality was subdued and sublimated, the mind refused to recognise external stimulants. Equally, once it had been released, everything was a stimulant.

Their joint activities had raised even her awareness. Perhaps it was because her own sex drive had been subdued by a marriage that had been less than fulfilling. Before marriage, her appetites had been healthy. Were they now in danger of going one step beyond?

Her body and emotions felt the need for sex, they

assessed every situation for potential. Last week, she had wondered about Mario, the head waiter, and fitted him into a fleeting fantasy in the restaurant.

Now she could not ride an elevator without wondering what it would be like to have sex between floors. She looked at the sleek white lines of the boats in the marina below and thought of fucking on the Thames below the walls of the Tower of London.

During her affair with Roger they had climaxed in unusual, semi-public and public places. It had excited her but she had known it was a phase of excitement which would end, that she could not go on fellating men on the back seats of buses for ever.

But even now, even reasoning with herself, the thought of it turned her on. That awful expression: turned on. But she *was* turned on, almost all the time, with her libido motivated by yearning, trepidation and even fear.

The fear of the unknown, the fear of the unthinkable. To be released from responsibility, to be subjected to whatever might be demanded of her, to submit herself without restraint.

Gina sipped the drink.

It was another hot day and she had on a Jean Muir white linen dress and sandals from Midas. Beneath it she wore only a bra and high-cut briefs. She had known the sun would shine through the dress, that men would be able to see the outline of her legs. That was one of the reasons she had worn it. As she stood before the window with the light behind her, she realised that Sam would also be able to see through the dress.

She remembered the kiss.

Sam wore blue silk. A long loose skirt and a floppy tunic

top that was gathered at her waist with a gold belt. The silk was fluid and deceptive but Gina had noticed that Sam was not wearing a bra. Part of the fluidity was caused by the sway of her breasts.

Blue suited Sam. Blonde hair and blue eyes, tanned ankles showing beneath the hem of the skirt.

The silk suit had probably come from a chain store or one of those markets she frequented in that part of the East End not yet destroyed by progress and redevelopment. Sam could make the most ordinary garment look as if it deserved a designer label.

Sam put the photocopied pages down and looked up. Their eyes locked for a long moment before Sam broke the connection by raising her glass and taking a drink.

'What do you think?' Gina said.

'I think I'm glad you didn't give me this while Mario was watching.'

Gina smiled tightly.

'The new diet is still working,' she said. 'I haven't been able to eat since I read it.'

Sam sat back on the couch. She drank more gin and tonic and stared at Gina over the rim of the glass.

'It all reads like fantasy,' she said.

Gina bit her lip.

'But it isn't.'

'I can't tell what's real and what isn't. Did this happen with Roger at the party? In the bedroom?'

Gina was acutely aware that her body was on display. For some reason, she wanted it to be on display. She wanted Sam to notice and to look at her.

'Let's not be euphemistic, Sam. Roger fucked me in the bedroom. In a way, I led him on. I could have avoided it. I allowed the situation to happen. I went into the bedroom with him. Then he fucked me.'

Sam's cheeks were flushed, her lips apart. The tip of her tongue peeked between them. She gulped before she spoke, in a low voice.

'You knelt over the bed and . . . he fucked you?'

Gina knew then. She knew from the blush in Sam's cheeks and the small thrill that went through her friend as she said that magic word. Gina was hooked on the sex, caught up in this unstoppable urge that gushed like a fresh-drilled well. Now she saw that Sam was hooked, too. On the journal. On the confessions and disclosures. On how much more?

'Yes. He made me come with his fingers.' Her smile was still tight. 'Roger was always considerate. He made sure I came first and then he came.'

Sam's lips trembled. She seemed in danger of spilling the drink she held.

'And Hugo watched?'

'Oh yes. I saw him in the mirror. He watched.'

Sam's eyes widened.

'You knew he was there?'

'I knew he was there and I knew he could stop it happening. He didn't want to. I didn't know at the time, but I didn't want him to, either.'

The blonde woman seemed to come out of a trance. She finished the drink and stood up.

'No wonder you seemed odd when you were leaving.'

Sam glanced away and went to the sideboard where bottles and an ice bucket sat.

'I wasn't feeling odd, Sam. I was feeling sex. I was sex. I was full of sex. It was oozing from me.' She almost chuckled. 'Like Roger's sperm was oozing from me.'

Gina gulped more of her drink and also went to the sideboard.

Sam said, 'The story you told Hugo. The story that happened at my wedding. Did it really happen?'

They were standing close together now and Gina could smell Sam's perfume. She wore Coco Chanel, always had. Looked good in their suits, too. She watched a nerve jump in Sam's neck as her friend poured gin.

'Roger fucked me in the cocktail bar and a waiter watched from behind the grille. Silently in the shadows. He hardly breathed because he didn't want us to notice him, except that we had noticed him. But no, the rest didn't happen. That was the fiction I moulded onto the fact. Like you told me to.' She reached past Sam and placed her glass down. 'Hugo liked it.'

Sam smiled nervously and, still holding the gin bottle, half turned to face Gina.

'I must admit, I liked it, too.'

They were very close. Gina could almost taste Sam's breath and she knew, now, why she had telephoned her friend with such urgency. It was not just the journal, it was the whole situation, the whole runaway experience. It was the kiss.

That moment when their mouths had met and they had kissed, not as friends but as lovers, had stayed with her on the fringes while she and her husband had done other things, but it had been waiting for an excuse to come back and demand its own conclusion. The entry in the journal had been a valid excuse. But it had still been an excuse.

Fear showed in Sam's eyes. It excited Gina more. She took the bottle from Sam and put it back on the sideboard and, as if by accident, their bodies brushed against each other. Sam's trembled.

It was almost as if their senses had moved into slow motion as Gina reached up and brushed the long blonde hair from Sam's face. Her fingers went into the hair, went behind her head and onto her neck. She raised her other hand and ran a finger down Sam's cheek to her parted lips.

'You are so beautiful, Sam. That kiss . . .'

She shook her head as if there were no words to describe what the kiss had meant. The surprise at how delicious it had been, at how new feelings had been stirred. Gina felt as if she had captured Sam with the strength of her gaze. As if the other woman had been pierced by her eyes and was unable to resist.

The fear was still there in Sam and released a wave of tenderness and love in Gina. Her face moved closer until they were, now, actually sharing the same breath. Their lips met, gently and without pressure. Sam's were dry and she licked them with the tip of her tongue and it met Gina's tongue and her eyes closed and Gina knew a friendship was over for the moment and a love affair was about to begin.

They moved easily into each other's arms, their softness complementing each other. Their mouths open, their tongues wrestled lazily. Sam still trembled but no longer from fear. She remained passive and Gina moved her hands over the slim body in her arms.

Why had no one told her it could be this good?

The silk enhanced Sam's curves. It tempted hands to slide and caress. Gina's hands slid and caressed. Her right hand moved over the softness of her buttocks. Their legs entwined and they rubbed themselves against each other's thighs. The kiss continued and became more lascivious.

Their tongues became more demanding.

Gina put her arm around Sam's waist and began to pull her towards the bedroom while their mouths were still meshed together. Sam's eyes opened again and showed fresh fear at the possibility of a consummation.

'You have no choice,' Gina whispered into her mouth. 'This has to be.'

Sam allowed herself to be led although she was still hesitant. At the doorway of the bedroom, Gina pushed the blonde girl ahead of her, but retained possession with a hand upon her breasts that were gloriously loose beneath the silk, and another on her hip.

She pushed Sam against the bedroom wall and pressed herself against her back, feeling the buttocks against her groin, the small pointed breasts in her palms.

Gina raised her hands to grip the V neck of the smock at the front and ripped it apart. Sam shuddered against her. The silk slid from her shoulders and pooled at her waist and wrists and now Gina held the naked breasts and kissed the back of her neck.

Sam was murmuring unintelligible words or noises, as if lost from reality, as if she wondered where she was and what was happening.

Gina pushed up the skirt impatiently until her hands found the silk of Sam's thighs. They touched her buttocks before they moved greedily around her hips and dipped into the creases where her thighs met her body. Fingers traced the edges of the panty line, slipping beneath the silk into the pubic curls. The fingers went slowly downwards and inwards, along the two sides of the triangle, all the way to their inevitable destination. Sam's vagina was dry and Gina pushed the panties to one side and stroked it gently.

The lips parted and accepted a greedy finger that dipped inside and discovered the wetness waiting to be released.

The blonde girl had continued to murmur and now the words made brief sense.

She said, 'Oh my God, oh my God . . .'

Gina pushed two fingers inside Sam. She had become sex again, where every tingling nerve-end was as sensitive as a clitoris. She had an urge to transfer the same feeling to Sam, to share its totality, to make Sam surrender and become one in sex with her.

The fingers forced a rhythm that made Sam cry out. Gina bit the back of Sam's neck and her free hand fondled her breasts. All the time, she thrust her groin against her buttocks as if she were a man.

Sam moaned. She raised her arms against the wall, a crucified victim on her way to heaven. The fingers were doing their work. Gina moved them up onto the clitoris and Sam twitched and bucked. The pace and suddenness of the attack had left them both without breath and without any thought other than sex.

The fingers worked and Gina licked an ear and Sam came, abruptly tipping into orgasm, shaking against the wall in Gina's harsh embrace, moans and sighs dribbling from her throat.

While her limbs were still twitching in the aftermath, Gina led her to the bed. She laid her down and stripped off her clothes. Naked, Sam looked vulnerable. Slim and girlish and wide-eyed. The wide eyes watched Gina as she discarded her own clothes and dropped them upon the floor.

Gina felt they could not stop to rationalise their actions, for if they did, they might not start again. She felt the need to continue and lay upon the bed alongside her naked friend, while Sam stared at her in shock.

They embraced properly and tenderness replaced the fury of a moment before. They kissed, long and gently, and their hands explored and Sam's eyes closed and shut out the doubts. Sam's touch was at first hesitant but when her fingers elicited soft groans of pleasure from Gina, she became bolder. With encouragement, she touched her seducer between the legs and entered Gina's vagina.

Female fingers, knowing fingers.

Gina's eyes now widened and she stared into Sam's face with surprise and she came.

A virginity lost, and so beautifully.

They brought each other to orgasm after orgasm in turn, with fingers and by joining their vaginas and letting their sex mouths make love to each other. They were close to being sated and swimming in sex when Gina slid down to cross the last frontier. Sam lay back without demur and let her go between her legs and suckle at her sex.

Hugo had written that he was unsure how he would react to performing such an act upon his wife. At moments when the memory of the kiss had activated her imagination, Gina had wondered the same. How would she react at performing the ultimate intimacy upon another woman?

The smell of sex as she nosed through the slicked pubic hair welcomed her. The smell, the texture, the taste and the wonderful complexity of tender flesh made this kiss as memorable as the first.

Gina consumed Sam's vagina, as sex had consumed her, and Sam orgasmed on her mouth. Gina refused to stop and the spasms never fully subsided before Sam orgasmed again.

Now Sam made her cease and dragged her back to kiss her and lick her own juices from Gina's lips. Now Sam slid down the bed, her wet mouth trailing over voluptuous and tingling flesh until it reached the waiting lips between Gina's thighs. She kissed, lips upon lips, and her tongue repaid the pleasure.

Gina sighed into orgasm.

Chapter 18

They must have slept. Gina awoke in bed covered by a duvet. The curtains had been closed and the light was diffused. Sam lay with her back to her. Her blonde hair spilled across the pillow.

Gina felt no embarrassment, only tenderness. She rolled against her friend and kissed her back. Sam was not asleep.

'How did it happen?' she whispered.

'I don't know. I'm glad it did.' Sam did not respond. 'Aren't you?'

'I'm frightened that it happened.'

'Why?'

'It makes me unsure.'

'About what?'

'My marriage. Me.'

'You're unsure about your sexuality?'

'Yes.'

Gina kissed her again.

'Don't be. This was sex. Loving sex. Because it was between two women doesn't matter. Don't try to categorise it, or isolate it.'

'It's difficult not to.'

'We're both victims of the journal, Sam. I've felt its

171

power growing. I thought I could control it but the other night I knew I couldn't.'

Sam turned onto her back. Her make-up had worn off during their love-making and she looked young and vulnerable. She turned her head on the pillow to look at Gina.

'You're not making sense,' she said.

'Don't worry. Sex has not sent me mad. But the journal is the catalyst. It allowed Hugo to discover sex. I hadn't realised it, but I had a lot of sexual energy stored up, too. The journal allowed it to be released. And you admitted the only relief you got was self-administered. You read the journal, you shared it.'

She smiled.

'I thought of you as a silent witness to what Hugo and I did but you were more than that. You were a participant. We discussed the journal, you and I. You advised about it. You read it and it gave you orgasms. You were part of it, Sam. And now the journal has developed its own impetus and we have become its victims.'

'Do you really believe this?'

'Totally. You had your chance to say no, to stop being involved. The kiss was the last warning.' She stared at Sam. 'Didn't you feel it?'

'Yes.'

'That was the last warning. You could still have escaped if you had wanted. You could have stopped it after that, like Hugo could have stopped Roger fucking me. Like I could have stopped it. But you wanted the vicarious thrill. You wanted the orgasms. You wanted to be part of it. After the kiss, this was inevitable.'

Sam looked at the ceiling.

'I suppose so. I suppose if not this, then something else. Me and Hugo?'

'Perhaps.'

'What now?'

'Now you decide if you want to stay involved.'

'I am involved. How can I stop?'

'Walk away. Don't read the journal any more. Don't see me.'

Sam turned her head to look into Gina's face again.

'I can't do that. I can't pretend this hasn't happened, either.'

'Will you want to do this again?'

'I don't know. Maybe doing it again will spoil it.'

Gina smiled.

'The memory of the kiss survived. I'll never forget it. I'll never forget this. I don't think it will spoil but I don't know if it can be planned. This happened. You can't fake spontaneity.'

'Perhaps the journal can.'

'Perhaps.'

'What will you do, Gina? Will you stay a victim?'

'Yes. I want to see where the journal takes us. Me and Hugo. Sometimes it frightens me, but fear is a great aphrodisiac. And it beats the hell out of lunch at Mario's.'

They both laughed and touched each other's faces with tenderness.

Sam said, 'What Hugo wrote in the journal. To be forced to do the unthinkable. Is that what you want?'

'I won't know until it happens. But I do know the possibility excites me.'

'To really be a victim? Of men, as well as the journal?'

'I suppose it's a question of interpretation. Like you said.

Submitting would be my decision. No one else's. That would make me a willing victim. The men aren't important, except as extras.' She kissed Sam's shoulder as the images filled her mind. 'They would be guests in my fantasy.'

'The journal talks about being dominated.'

'I've had dreams about it. Some of them were not pleasant. Others were strangely fascinating. I woke up wanting an orgasm. If it really happened, I would hate it. But this way, the way Hugo might plan it, I just don't know.'

Sam said, 'You want to be freed of responsibility?'

'I feel that's the direction I'm going anyway. That both Hugo and I are going.'

'It sounds dangerous.'

'I know. That's what attracts me.'

Sam said, 'What if Hugo asks you about us? Will you tell him?'

'I would like to tell him. Would you object?'

'I don't know.' Sam thought about it. 'No. I wouldn't object. What you have already told him is part fiction and part fact. He might like to believe this happened, but he would never be sure.'

'Unless he tried to arrange a repeat performance at which he could be present.'

'Would he want to?'

'Two women together? Hugo wrote about the ultimate female fantasy, well this is the ultimate male fantasy. To watch and then join in.'

Sam smiled to herself, as if imagining such a situation.

'I still don't object. You can tell him, if he asks. I'm not as deeply hooked as you are.'

'Don't be too sure.' Gina laughed and stroked the back

of Sam's neck. 'I have a confession to make.'

'After what we've just done? I can't imagine what it is.'

'I bit the back of your neck. I looked when I woke up. You can see the teeth marks. I'm afraid it's likely to bruise.'

Sam laughed.

'My hair will cover it.'

'When does Brian get back?'

'Two days.'

'Won't he notice?'

'I doubt it.'

'If he does? What if he asks about it?'

'I'll say you gave it to me in a moment of passion. I could start telling him stories. Perhaps it would give him a moment of passion.'

Gina's look was serious.

'Perhaps it would. Perhaps it will.'

'I don't know if I could stand it if Brian started writing a journal.'

'Maybe you should just let him read the one we've got?'

Sam's eyes widened again. She looked like a sixth-former who had been offered the end of term exam results the day before the exam.

'Now, that's something I might consider.'

Chapter 19

Gina was surprised that she and Hugo were able to have ordinary sex without the need for talk, fantasy or the fuck word. During the next four days, they made love satisfactorily on three occasions. Each time it happened in bed when they had retired for the night and each time they both orgasmed.

In a way, it was reassuring that they could be ordinary, but she was aware that the experience was not as rewarding as their stage-managed performances.

Perhaps they needed this trough to allow nerve ends to repair themselves. Perhaps they needed anticipation before the next stage of their adventure. They had already moved on from using alcohol as an excuse and Hugo no longer needed to be directed in performing oral sex or coaxed into allowing Gina to take him in her mouth.

Their normal sex life had blossomed because of the game she had started and which the journal had taken over. They did not, of course, talk or acknowledge either the existence of the game or the journal. Both waited to be resumed.

Meanwhile, Gina was discovering that normal was no longer enough.

Sunday it rained and they drank wine with lunch and continued drinking wine during the afternoon because there seemed no reason not to. By early evening they were both tired and, by consensus, went to bed. They slept for a little while, both naked. When Gina awoke, Hugo was lying against her back and touching her. She felt the tension in his hands and knew this time it would not be ordinary.

She moved to let him know she was aware of what he was doing.

He kissed her neck.

'I can't stop thinking about the party,' he said. 'The night you kissed Sam.'

'Mmmm.'

She squirmed as if the memory was pleasant.

'It seemed like you enjoyed it?' he said.

'I did.

'Did Sam?'

'Yes.'

'How can you be so certain?'

'I could tell. Besides, she said so afterwards.'

'You talked about it?'

'Yes.'

'Where?'

'At her apartment.'

'When?'

'A few days ago.'

'I thought you lunched?'

'Not this time. We wanted somewhere to talk and Brian was away.'

He kissed her ear. His erection stiffened between the curves of her buttocks.

'Have you kissed women before?' he said.

'Not like that.'

'Not at school?'

Gina smiled to herself. She could easily make up a story about schoolgirls, if she wanted, but she preferred the danger of telling him the truth.

'No. Not at school.'

His sigh was of disappointment.

'Why did you kiss Sam?'

'It was an urge. I was suddenly aware of how attractive she was and that gender didn't really matter. My feelings of sex mattered. I was aroused.'

'Why were you aroused?'

'I knew you were taking me home to fuck me. Perhaps I decided to kiss her to shock you, I don't really know. Maybe that was my excuse. But when I did kiss her, I enjoyed it. You saw how much I enjoyed it.'

His lips moved over her shoulder.

'Have you kissed her since?'

'Yes. At the apartment a few days ago.'

'Why?'

'Because I wanted to. Because I couldn't forget how much I'd enjoyed kissing her the first time. Because I knew it would excite you when I told you.'

'It does.' He kissed her and rubbed his erection against her. 'It excites me.'

'It excited me.'

'Did Sam kiss you back?'

'Oh yes.'

'What happened?'

'I ripped her clothes off and fucked her.'

His erection jumped against her softness.

'You did what?'

'I fucked her. I sucked her and fucked her and she did the same to me.'

His breath quivered in her ear.

'Did she come?'

'Many times.'

'Did you?'

'Even more times.'

'Tell me,' he whispered hoarsely, moving her legs, putting his erection into the mouth of her vagina. 'Tell me.'

He sank upon her back and she told him as he groaned and moved upon her.

After the telling came the re-telling in small segments so he could re-enact them. She didn't mind. He accepted the challenge of giving her more orgasms than Sam had. When she relaxed with the surfeit of sex, he became frustrated and changed his technique from loving tenderness to harsh demands.

He moved her about the bed with new fire and an edge of brutality that aroused her afresh. He pushed her head down and made her suck him, he turned her onto her hands and knees until she was almost double and took her harshly from behind. He pinned her down with his body, his penis rubbing in her hair, while he sucked between her legs.

Gina responded and became animated until they were almost fighting and she raked his back with her fingernails. Hugo pounded into her, staring into her face with wide eyes and gasping mouth, and she felt between them to touch herself to one last orgasm as he came.

They slept fitfully afterwards. She dreamed that the journal had grown in size until it became a Hollywood device that held people and places as well as words. Each page turned revealed a full-colour illustration that became alive and filled the screen of her mind.

Even though she knew the plot of the different pages they still held her in thrall with the possibility that the ending might change or a new character might be introduced. These were plots that were new and yet familiar. In some she was an actress, in others she became a victim.

She wore a period costume, she was back at Roger's party. The situations were many and varied. One image settled.

Gina sat naked behind the desk in the study reading the journal. She was fixed by a camera on a screen. The camera captured her image from the front. Her breasts quivered as she read. Her right arm moved rhythmically in her lap, her hand hidden behind the desk.

The camera zoomed slowly in for a close-up and dipped beneath the desk. It focused on her fingers as she pleasured herself. Closer and closer until the image filled the screen and she used her left hand to spread the lips of her vagina while the fingers of her right hand continued to masturbate. Closer still, between the swollen pink lips of her sex, and deep into that colourful maelstrom and now she was the camera and she had been swallowed by sex.

Gina woke up and tried to hold onto the fragments of the dream. Had it been allegorical? A warning or a welcome? The fragments were too flimsy to keep in her mind. Hugo stirred and they blew away.

They had created their own night by closing the curtains and going to bed. The shadows had deepened now that night had really come.

'Sam has problems,' Gina said.

She stared at the ceiling and wondered what had prompted her to tell Hugo. Sometimes it was best not to look for reasons, but to follow instinct.

He rolled onto his side and she felt him looking at her profile.

'What sort of problems?'

'With Brian.'

'Divorce?'

'No. She still loves him. She says he still loves her. But they no longer make love.'

He did not speak for a while.

'Is he having an affair?' he asked.

'No. At least, she doesn't think so. She says they've just got out of the habit of having sex.'

'She's a beautiful woman.'

'Yes.'

'How could anyone get out of the habit . . .?'

The sentence trailed off. Perhaps he was thinking of his own problems before the journal – before the game.

Gina said, 'It happens. Brian's greatest commitment is to his job. He's an influential man. Influence and power – a heady combination. Perhaps he doesn't need sex.'

'But Sam does?'

'She has sex. Alone. She gives herself sex.'

'It's not the same.'

'I know.'

Did he know what she meant? He stroked her arm. She was sure that he did.

'Is there an answer?'

'I don't know.'

'If it would do any good, I can talk to him,' he said. 'But how am I supposed to know?'

'Exactly.'

'Besides, he'd be offended that Sam had told other people. Even you.'

'Yes, he would.'

They lay in silence.

He said, 'You want to help her, don't you?'

'Yes.'

'Do you believe what she says? That they've got out of the habit?'

'Yes. I believe it. I believe it can happen. After six years of marriage.'

'Six years is not a long time.'

'It is if the passion is not renewed.'

'What do you mean?'

'Perhaps their love-making became a routine. Part of their routine. Perhaps it became a chore instead of an excitement. Something that had to be done. So they adjusted their routine and stopped doing it. Like smoking.'

'You make it sound like a cold-blooded decision.'

'I didn't mean to. Sam said it got embarrassing – having sex after they had not had it for a long time. It was less embarrassing not to do it at all. They now have separate rooms.'

They lapsed into another silence.

Hugo said, 'Do you think it is possible to renew their passion?'

'It might be.'

'I hope they do.'

'So do I.'

Gina still did not know why she had confided in Hugo. In doing so, had she broken the confidence placed in her by Sam? She did not think so. She thought of her bedroom conversations with her husband as sacrosanct, as if they were confessionals. They would go no further, except, perhaps, into the journal, and it was the journal she thought might help Sam and Brian to renew their passion.

'It's half past nine,' he said. He sat up and stretched. 'Do you want wine or coffee?'

She turned her head to smile up into his face.

'I would like a cup of tea.'

'Tea it will be.' He bent to kiss her. 'In here or through there?'

'Through there. I'm not tired any more. Perhaps there's something on television.'

He got out of bed. His sexual awakening had made him more comfortable and more aware of his body. He had become more manly.

'Hungry?' he said.

'Yes. That, too.'

'I'll fix something.'

He was now capable of fixing all her bodily wants.

Gina felt guilty that her marriage had blossomed while Sam's had slipped into torpor. But surely the passion between Sam and Brian was latent? Perhaps it only needed the slightest adjustment to re-activate it.

Chapter 20

Hugo wrote in the journal of his surprise and delight at Gina's seduction of Sam. He re-told the episode in his own way and Gina realised he was developing his own style. Once again, it aroused her to read about the encounter from a different perspective.

She had wondered how he would react. After all, she had been instigator and seductress. Would he see her behaviour as something to fear? He did not.

This was not infidelity. This was love between two close friends, an encounter that had, perhaps been waiting to happen for years.

Somehow, sex between women seems natural. Far more natural than sex between men. Or is this homophobic prejudice? I certainly have no desire to indulge in sex with another man, the bodies of women are infinitely superior for that purpose. I also do not see the relationship between Gina and Sam as a threat.

Sam was in need of comfort and Gina provided it, but my wife still loves me and Sam still loves Brian, although their relationship appears to be in a parlous state.

When Gina told me Sam and Brian no longer made love, I felt closer to the problem than anyone else ever could because, I now realise, Gina and I were almost in the same position because of my ignorance.

I had sex in brief couplings that provided me with a release, but did not satisfy Gina. By no stretch of the imagination could it have been described as making love. Yet now I could take her in public while screaming obscenities into her face and that would be making love; mad, violent love without reason, love for the sake of sex, sex for the sake of love.

All concepts intermingle in passion. I have said this before. Romance, love, lust, fucking.

It is possible, I should imagine, to achieve great excitement fucking a beautiful stranger with total abandonment. But when it is a woman you know and love that you are fucking, when you are fucking each other, that adds an extra element. That becomes the ultimate combination of head, heart and prick. That was why watching Roger fuck Gina at the party was such a release.

If I had watched him fuck another woman I would have been excited. But he wasn't fucking another woman, he was fucking Gina my wife, the woman I love and the woman who loves me. That was an experience that transcended excitement. Although he was the seducer, he was of no account in our relationship. For him, the seduction and the sex was one-dimensional. For me it was so much more.

But I am digressing. Or am I?

It is appalling that Sam and Brian have forgone the physical part of their relationship. Perhaps it died of neglect, of lack of stimulation. Perhaps Gina is right and it needs a renewal of passion.

Sam would be receptive, that is certain, but how to open Brian's eyes? How to re-awaken his lust? Perhaps Gina and I can help. At least, we must try.

Trying will be a tributary to the river I am following. The river that I hope will lead to the source of all pleasure. Is there such a thing or am I on a fool's errand? Will one adventure simply lead to another and another; adventures without end? If that is the case, will I know when to stop?

Gina must be the judge. She is the final arbiter for it is my love for her that drives me. My desire to see another man make love to her, to fuck her, is based on love, for the jealousy and pain and lust such an experience would arouse would be an overdose of love.

Or has sex become a drug? The ultimate drug. And I an addict.

I do not care if that is the case because it does not invalidate anything else I have said. For this journal is a testimony to love as well as sex. I committed my soul to it at the start and I have no intention of abandoning my dreams. I intend to achieve all I set out to achieve.

This journal has become my soul and guide. The book of law which I shall follow. Which we shall follow, Gina and I, until we know it has served its purpose and I can make the final entry.

But not yet.

When? Wondered Gina. When?

It was reassuring that they shared the same excitements and doubts and that, in the jumble of thoughts committed to paper with a few corrections, he still maintained she held the sway on how far they should go.

But she didn't know how far she wanted to go. Like her husband, each development made her hungry for more. Sex between them really had become a drug and she was happy to be hooked.

Gina took the latest photocopies to the restaurant in Knightsbridge. She and Sam had agreed on the telephone to resume their weekly lunch date and, by inference, resume normal relations.

They hadn't seen each other since the day in the apartment overlooking the Thames. Sam was already at the restaurant and, it appeared to Gina, had fortified herself for the encounter with two large glasses from the first bottle of wine.

Sam blushed when Gina kissed her on the cheek.

'Blushing suits you,' said Gina. 'It makes you look young.'

'And foolish? I thought we'd talked it all out, but it still feels strange.'

'To be here instead of in bed?'

Gina was being deliberately blunt. Her gaze was frank as it held Sam's eyes.

'I suppose so. Last week, it . . . it takes some getting used to.'

'Me too.'

She reached across the table and touched Sam's hand. Sam smiled and the blush receded.

'I thought we'd talked it out. Like mature people do. But the next day when I woke up, it was like a hangover. The doubts were back. About all sorts of things.'

'I know. It was the same with me.'

'I mean, talking about it seemed to put it in its place. In perspective. We boxed it in with words. But the next day, I'd forgotten the words, the reasons.' She laughed at herself. 'When I went to the office, I wondered if people could tell. You know Julie? Gay Julie? I wondered if she could tell. Then I wondered if I was staring too hard at her. I worried then, in case she thought I fancied her.' She shook her head. 'Then I tried to work out if I did fancy her.'

Gina laughed and Sam giggled.

Sam said, 'I mean, it was crazy.'

Gina said, 'Do you fancy her?'

'No. Julie is a lovely girl, but I don't.'

'Do you fancy me?'

Their looks were frank again.

'Right at this moment, no,' Sam said. 'Right at this moment, I love you as my friend. As I always have. But I don't want to go to bed with you.'

'Signoras?'

Mario was standing by the table and they were still holding hands. They let go and Gina suppressed a giggle and picked up the menu.

'Chicken and salad,' she said.

'As always,' said Mario.

'As always,' she repeated.

Sam said, 'Minestrone, garlic bread and spaghetti bolognese.'

Mario nodded and left the table.

Gina said, 'You've regained your appetite.'

'It's the best minestrone in London. It's a sin not to eat it.'

'And the rest?'

'You're just jealous.'

'That's true.'

The banter relaxed them.

'Have you any more pages for me?'

'Yes. Do you want them now or later?'

'Let's eat first.'

'Afraid they'll spoil your appetite?'

'Perhaps.'

'Or are you still considering whether you want them?'

Sam smiled.

'It's a bit late for backing out. I want them.'

They ate and moved onto the second bottle of wine. When the last dish was cleared, Gina took the photostats from her bag and handed them across the table.

She watched her friend read for a moment, but could interpret nothing from her expression. She looked out of the window at the people and the traffic in the street. She sipped her wine but remained distracted because she was worried how Sam might react after discovering what she had told Hugo.

Sam shuffled the pages together, folded them and reached for her own bag. She put them inside.

Gina said, 'Are you angry?'

'No. I said you could tell him.'

'But the rest?'

'The rest is part of it. Isn't it?'

'That's what I thought. But I was worried.'

'No need to be.' Sam's smile was meant to be reassuring but looked fragile. 'It's just that reading about it, reading that I've got problems, makes me feel a bit vulnerable. A bit like an old maid.'

'That's how I felt when I confessed to you, right at the

start. About me and Hugo. I was so unsure.'

Sam nodded.

'Sex can be a bastard, can't it?' she said.

'Yes.'

'The bastard in the family no one talks about. And at the same time, sex can be as wonderful as last week at the apartment.'

Gina smiled. 'That was rather good, wasn't it?'

'In the journal, Hugo says I was in need of comfort. Is that what you thought, Gina? Is that why it happened? To comfort me?'

'It happened because I couldn't resist it, and neither could you. Bugger comfort. I was desperate to take you to bed.'

Sam took her fervour as a compliment and regained her good humour.

She said, 'I think Hugo gets an A-plus for effort. His descriptions are riveting. Not necessarily accurate, but riveting. I'm glad I ate first. I would've lost my appetite.

'You're still hooked?'

'Aren't we all?'

'Yes. We are.' Gina took a drink of wine and licked her lips, almost in anticipation. 'I wonder where the journal will take us next?'

'I hope it's not all going to be down a river. I'm not a very good swimmer.' They chuckled. 'Hugo's language does get a bit rich at times, doesn't it? I think he's much more effective when he sticks to the Anglo-Saxon. Fuck and suck suit him far more.'

Gina said, 'Is Brian at home?'

'Yes. His next trip is two weeks. Singapore.'

'Why not suggest going with him?'

'He would find the suggestion bizarre. Besides, he wouldn't have a clue what to do with me. I would be an encumbrance.'

'A beautiful encumbrance. If you went, it might make you more inclined to have extra-marital affairs. Heat and sweat and gin slings at Raffles. I'm sure there'd be many opportunities in Singapore.'

'I think not. I'm not interested in seeking solace in the arms of handsome Asians and Orientals, no matter how well versed in the Kama Sutra.'

'You want Brian, right?'

'Right.'

'I wonder if Hugo will get in touch with him.'

Sam shrugged.

'I admire his intentions but I don't know if he can do any good. Perhaps the key to salvation is here.' She patted her handbag. 'In the pages of the journal, as you suggested. In the meantime, I await future episodes with interest. Not to mention my tongue hanging out.'

'Me too.'

'Have you another story, if Hugo asks?'

'Of course.'

'Perhaps he's past stories. Perhaps what he wants now is action.'

'He still likes stories.'

'And you?'

'I like them, too.'

'What else is there to teach him?'

Gina shrugged and smiled enigmatically.

'The practices of Sodom? The philosophies of de Sade?'

'Buggery and sado-masochism? Not your style, Gina.'

'How do you know?'

Sam put her head to one side and stared at her quizzically.

'We are back to bastard sex again, aren't we? Even us. The bastard child about whom we mustn't speak.'

Gina nodded.

'Even us,' she said. 'No wonder relationships break down. We can talk about going to bed together but draw a line at sodomy.'

'Embarrassment is a terrible thing.'

'I think I'm beyond embarrassment.' Gina smiled. 'To save you asking, I have had sex the Greek way.'

'Beyond embarrassment but not euphemisms.'

Gina laughed.

'Touché.'

'And bondage and pain?' asked Sam.

'There was a man in my past who enjoyed tying me up.'

'You let him?'

'It was quite stimulating, being helpless and at the mercy of his whims.'

'And a bit dangerous.'

'That too. It's quite a commitment to let someone tie you to a bed. But I knew him pretty well.'

'Did he do anything outrageous?'

'Yes.'

'What?'

Sam's eyes were wide with expectation.

'He left me tied up while he went to the corner shop for cigarettes.' Sam started laughing. 'It wasn't funny,' Gina said. 'He could've been knocked down by a bus. Then what would I have done?'

'Were you cross?'

'At first I was, then I became frightened. What if someone else came in? It was his flat. What if he'd given a key to a friend? What if he came back with an entire football team? When you're helpless and tied to a bed your mind can play tricks from behind a blindfold.'

'A blindfold as well?'

Gina grinned.

'The sex was pretty incredible though. Fear builds great tension. He had to put his hand over my mouth when I came because I was yelling so loud.'

'What a sheltered life I've led,' Sam said.

'I don't believe it.'

'The closest I've been to bondage is getting locked in the loo at Euston.'

'Who with?'

'Alone. Bondage is an alien concept.'

A recent thought came back to Gina.

'You've worn sexy underwear, haven't you?'

'Well, yes, but I don't see the connection.'

'I often think the appeal of black underwear is because it looks like bondage. The straps of a garter belt and brassiere? Stockings like thigh boots? High heels of domination?'

'Stop!' Sam held up her hands in mock horror. 'This is too much psychology for a poor editor to understand.'

'Even one who studied the subject for a year?'

'I never qualified, remember? And we never got this far into sex. If we had I might have stuck at it. No, save it for the book. It has just the right degree of sincerity and sensationalism. Maybe we can do publicity pictures of you in black underwear?'

'You think that would be effective?'

'It was effective on Hugo, why not the general public?'

'Perhaps we should test the theory on Mario?'

They both looked across the restaurant and immediately caught the head waiter's eye. Sam motioned that they wanted the bill.

Sam said, 'You covered buggery and bondage. What about pain?'

'Pain has never appealed to me.'

'Me neither. I hope it doesn't appeal to Hugo. Especially after he's tied you to the bedpost.'

Chapter 21

On the face of it, Hugo's suggestion to help Sam and Brian seemed to be less than inspired. He said they should invite them round for supper.

Hugo made the suggestion when they were in bed. In the comfort of their confessional.

'Supper?' Gina was sceptical. 'I thought they needed something a little more exotic than supper. Maybe we could lace Brian's drink with Spanish Fly.'

'I think supper is safest,' he said. 'Without the Spanish Fly.'

'What are we going to do? Show them a blue movie?'

'I don't think you're taking this seriously.'

'Sorry.'

'Sam and Brian need to rediscover their passion for each other. We can't force that to happen. All we can try to do is create the right sort of circumstances so they can make their own discoveries.'

'I suppose so.'

She lay on her back and stared at the ceiling in the dark.

'I've given it some thought,' said Hugo, in his professional voice. 'Brian no longer sees Sam as a lover, only as a wife. His perceptions need changing. He needs to be persuaded to see her as the sexual and sensual woman that she really is. Do you agree?'

'You're beginning to sound a little pompous, but yes, I agree.'

He kissed her naked shoulder and laughed.

'I am, aren't I? I'll try not to.'

'You're right, though. I suppose some men get used to their wives like they get used to the furniture. They become part of the home. They take them for granted.'

'You don't believe love lasts?'

'Oh, I think it lasts. But I think it changes. Like it does in any relationship between a man and a woman. Lovers become companions.'

'Will it change between us?'

'It already has.' She wondered how much she should say, even here, in their confessional. 'It's got better.'

'It will get better still.'

'But it didn't for Sam and Brian. It hasn't for lots of others.'

'You talk as if sex is bound to die if two people get married,' he said.

'I don't mean that. Sex can stay in a marriage but usually it changes. In a new relationship, every touch is electric. But after living with someone for a few years the mystery goes. The sex becomes mechanical. Sometimes, it stops altogether.'

'Perhaps people need refresher courses.'

'You've got something there. Maybe you could run classes from the clinic?' Gina thought of Sam's fantasy of marketing the journal as a textbook and herself as a television expert. 'I could be your therapist.'

'What are you suggesting? I teach the theory and you

give practical demonstrations?'

She smiled in the darkness. 'If you like.'

He nuzzled her neck. 'What an interesting idea.'

She still didn't know what he hoped might happen if they invited Sam and Brian to supper.

'Sam and Brian? she said.

'Sam and Brian.' He kissed her shoulder. 'Samantha is a beautiful woman. She wants sex with her husband. It's Brian we should concentrate on. He has to be made to see her sexuality. He has to be seduced.'

'I thought the same thing. I wondered why she hadn't seduced him herself.'

'Fear,' Hugo said. 'Fear of rejection. How would she feel if she tried and failed?'

Gina remembered all Hugo had written in the journal about his own fear of failure.

'Terrible,' she said. 'She would feel terrible. It could destroy what was left of the marriage.'

'Sam has to be able to display her sexuality in a way that looks as if it is for her own benefit, not her husband's. Her sexuality has to show as a natural part of her being, that other people recognise. Brian has to be present, but he has to be incidental. Sam must express herself as a sensual woman and Brian has to be there to see it.'

'You're slipping into pompous again.' She turned her head and kissed his nose in the dark to soften the criticism. 'And, as a plan, it seems a bit vague.'

Gina looked back at the ceiling and he stroked her arm.

'It has to be,' he said. 'There can be no plan. There can be guidance, there can even be props: underwear, perfume, the right dress. But you can't plan spontaneity and this has to be spontaneous. It has to develop of its own volition.'

She agreed with him about spontaneity. That was what had made sex with Sam so wonderful.

Hugo added, 'We can provide the circumstances but the situation has to create itself.'

He sounded like his journal. But he would, wouldn't he? She smiled at the ceiling.

'Pompous, but I understand what you mean,' she said.

'I'm sorry. It's the way I am at times.'

'It's an endearing trait. At times. And you talk sense.'

'We can at least try. If it doesn't work, nothing will have been lost.' He kissed her shoulder again. 'If it's all as vague as you suggest, they won't even notice we've been scheming.'

'We'll invite them to supper. And we'll scheme.'

His hand moved over her body and caressed a breast.

'Would you mind terribly if, when they are here, I flirt a little with Sam?'

Gina turned her head on the pillow and looked into the shadowed face that lay alongside her own.

'Flirt a little?'

'Jealousy could arouse Brian.'

She kissed him on the nose.

'Flirt to your heart's content. Maybe I'll get jealous, too. I think I'd like to be jealous.'

'Perhaps you can show affection for Sam, as well?'

His eyes were white discs in the dark.

'The kiss?' she whispered.

'Perhaps.'

Gina looked back at the ceiling. She tingled at the

thought of kissing Sam in front of both Hugo and Brian. Could it be done in such a way that would be both innocent and sensual? In such a way that the kiss could be dismissed as playfulness and yet incite?

Hugo moved closer to her and she felt his penis against her thigh. it was heavy but not erect. His right hand moved over her, stroking her breasts lethargically before moving down her gently curved stomach.

He kissed her neck and his words were breathed into her ear.

'That's enough of Sam and Brian,' he said. 'Let's talk about us.'

'Us?'

'You. The past. Tell me something from the past. Something that happened before I knew you.'

His fingers were playing in her pubic hair. She arched her back.

'A love affair?'

'A lust affair.'

'About being fucked?'

His penis stiffened against her.

'Yes. About being fucked.'

'All right. But promise you won't blame me?'

'I won't blame you.'

He absolved her in advance with a kiss in her ear.

'Even though when I think of it I am ashamed?'

His erection got firmer and his breathing became heavier.

'Of course not. I won't blame you. It's in the past. Tell me. Please.'

Gina felt the power of her skills. She considered the story she had rehearsed in advance and knew it would send him wild. It had aroused her as she created the narrative and choreographed the scenes.

'All right.' She paused as if in thought. What else was there to teach him? 'When I left university,' she began, 'I was pretty naive in the ways of the world. I'd had student affairs and thought I knew everything about sex and men.' She sighed. 'Pretty naive.'

She paused on purpose.

'Go on,' he said.

'I went straight into public relations. A good company in the West End. All sorts of clients, show business and corporate. I was in the offices one day when a particularly wealthy client came in. An Arab. Oil money.

'He was immaculately dressed. Armani suit, Gucci shoes. a good-looking man of about forty. Dark hair and moustache. He had two large companions, both Arabs but dressed in Western clothes. They were his bodyguards.

'Tariq made a point of introducing himself to me before he went in to see my boss. After he'd gone, my boss said Tariq had requested that I be assigned to him. He had social events he wished to organise, he said, and needed help.

'It wasn't strictly PR but I thought it could be a good career move. I didn't realise what he had in mind.'

His fingers dipped between her legs and discovered her little beast. She groaned.

'Do you want me to go on? Do you want me to tell you what happened?'

'Yes.' His fingers worked persuasively. 'Tell me.'

Her little beast said: Tell him. But tell him slowly.

'He was staying at The Savoy. He had suites of rooms. That afternoon we went shopping. We travelled in a Rolls

Royce. He said he wanted to buy presents for his wife. He said she was my size and he asked me to model dresses and clothes, which I did.

'It was quite an experience because he was treated like royalty wherever we went. And because I was with him, so was I. He was the perfect gentleman: charming and witty and patient. He bought underwear and shoes for his wife. Boxes of things. He said in all things we were the same size. That was why he had asked for my help.

'We went back to The Savoy and he insisted I stay and have dinner with him. I could wear some of the new clothes, he said. I still didn't see anything wrong in what he suggested. But first, he said, we needed a glass of champagne after all the shopping. We had more than a glass but I didn't really notice because he was so charming. So flattering.

'We drank champagne and talked. Just the two of us. Then he rang a bell and an Arab maid came into the room and he spoke to her in her own language. He told me she would prepare a bath for me. That she would look after me. When the maid came back, I went with her into a bedroom with its own bathroom. Having her with me made me feel secure, even though she spoke no English. I had a bath.

'When I came out of the bathroom, my clothes had gone. new clothes were laid out on the bed, things we had bought that afternoon. A whole outfit was there. Shoes, dress, underwear, stockings. I didn't usually wear stockings but now I was expected to wear them and it made me feel nervous. For the first time, I felt nervous.'

Gina had taken care with presenting the background. Whether fact or fiction, she had learned that detail helped Hugo's imagination.

Hugo said, 'What colour was the dress?'

'White. It was white silk.'

'And the underwear?'

'White. And white stockings and white shoes.'

He groaned and rubbed his erection against her hip. His fingers plied her furrow and her little beast was happy.

'Go on,' he said.

'The maid came in and I asked where my clothes were but she didn't understand. She pointed to the clothes on the bed. Again, I was reassured by her presence and so I dressed. The garter belt and the stockings felt strange. They made me aware that I was a woman. They made me feel nervous. When I looked at myself in the mirror, the silk of the dress was so sheer, I could see the outline of my underwear as I moved.'

Gina licked her lips. She suddenly had second thoughts about the story. Hugo might be scandalised if he believed it to be true or disappointed if he thought it too extreme to have really happened.

'Go on,' he said.

'There was nothing else for me to wear and the maid ushered me into another room. A large room with soft lights and candles. Arabic music was playing softly in the background. Large cushions and rugs were spread everywhere. Carpets and tapestries hung on the walls. Incense burned. The effect was disorientating. Tariq was there, but he no longer wore Western clothes. He wore a long white cotton robe and sandals.

'I tried not to move too much because of the way the dress clung but he seemed not to notice. He was still charming, still witty. He said he hoped I didn't mind but he had brought an Arabian night to rainy London.

'He made me laugh and put me at my ease. We drank more champagne and sat on cushions at a low table. The maid brought food. Oysters, chicken, spiced snacks. We ate with our fingers. Some of the tastes were strange. We drank more champagne and I relaxed.

'The maid cleared the food. The music and the incense and the way we lay on the cushions made me lethargic. We were now drinking a liqueur that was rich and delicious. I had never tasted anything like it before. Tariq lit a cannabis cigarette. I recognised the smell. I shared it with him and relaxed even more.

'I was feeling good. Then Tariq opened a packet of white powder and poured it on the table. He made lines with it and used a gold straw to sniff the powder up his nose. I knew what it was. I'd never had any before, had never wanted any. But right then it seemed the most natural thing in the world to try it. Tariq helped. We giggled a lot. And I snorted the powder. And I lost control of my feelings.'

Gina still had the chance to change her story. To abbreviate it, adapt it to a lesser conclusion. But the uncertainty of how Hugo would react excited her. It was the fear element again. Besides, the story excited her as well.

'What happened?' Hugo said.

'I suppose it had been his intention all along.'

'To drug you?'

'Yes. To make me incapable of saying no.'

'Were you? Incapable of saying no?'

'I was incapable of speech.'

'What did he do? Tell me.'

'The next thing I knew I was lying on my back and he was kissing me. His hands were touching me. The dress was around my waist and a hand was between my legs. I think I became aware of what was happening when he pushed his fingers inside me.'

Hugo groaned and pressed himself against her side. His fingers slid into her.

'The terrible thing is, his fingers felt good,' she said. 'I couldn't speak but I made noises. I moaned and groaned because of his fingers.'

'Oh my God.'

'Then I noticed his two bodyguards were in the room. They wore robes like his. They were watching.'

'What happened?'

'Tariq ripped the dress down the front. He ripped it open. He ripped my panties. Pulled them off. He had me first and then his bodyguards . . .'

'They had you?'

'Yes.'

'How? How did they have you?'

'Every way possible. They did whatever they wanted.'

'Every way?'

'Tariq turned me over. He used oil on my bottom. He sodomised me.'

Hugo convulsed against her side and then became immobile. His fingers became still inside her vagina. Gina wondered if she had gone too far this time. Slowly he let out his breath.

'He sodomised you?'

'Yes.'

'How?'

'Like this.'

Chapter 22

Hugo telephoned Brian and invited him and Sam to supper. He insisted they come by taxi. Alcohol was no aphrodisiac but it could loosen stuffed shirts, Hugo explained to Gina. She smiled and refrained from saying it had certainly loosened his when he had thought she was intoxicated.

When the date had been fixed, Gina called Sam and they met for a drink at a pub near Sloane Square. They sat on high stools in an alcove and drank spritzers. The pub was busy with noise, shoppers, tourists and workers on their lunch break.

'Why here?' Sam asked.

'Neutral ground and other reasons.'

'Sounds like the title of a thriller.'

'I'm fed up of Mario watching us blush and giggle. I feel he's so much part of it, he could write the foreword to the text book.'

'And the other reasons?'

'There's an underwear shop I want to show you round the corner.'

'Planning my trousseau, as well?'

'Certainly not. But this place is a bit more exciting than Marks and Sparks.'

'What on earth do you think is going to happen at this supper party?'

'Nothing amazing. But it's as well to be prepared.'

'You mean I should dress like a boy scout?'

'If that'll turn Brian on, why not?'

They both laughed.

Sam said, 'I wonder what he'd say if he came home and found me playing with my woggle?'

'He might like it.'

'Has Hugo been playing with his journal again?'

'Of course.'

'Do I get to read it now or later?'

Gina looked around the bustling pub.

'I wouldn't have thought this was the place to read erotica.'

'It's ideal. All this male jostling on the way to the loo. When I've finished we can go down the King's Road and find a couple of Chelsea football supporters.'

'Now you're talking serious sado-masochism.'

Gina handed her the photocopied pages and concentrated on her white wine and soda while Sam read.

Hugo had gone straight into re-telling her tale of a thousand and one indignities at the hands of an Arab sheikh and his henchmen. He had embraced the challenge of recreating the scene with enthusiasm, although his language had drifted a little into the vernacular.

Previously, he had contented himself with fuck and suck but now his use of colloquialisms had become much wider and earthier. As well as Anglo-Saxon, he was using middle-English and Germanic vulgar slang. Being an English graduate provided Gina with a different way of assessing her husband's literary style.

The story had been effective, both on the night she told it and when he'd come to enter it in the journal. The handwriting became an erratic scrawl in the middle of the re-telling, calmed down, and degenerated once more towards the end. From its irregularities, she judged he had had to break off twice to restore his equilibrium.

Afterwards, as always, the entry became reflective about the philosophy and progress of his sexual awakening.

Gina surprised me again. Shocked me. But what a wonderful shock. What a wonderful new delight. A new method of assault in the armoury of love.

The amazing part about her telling me these stories is my willingness to believe. Could it be true? Her details are precise, as if plucked from memory, and yet the content is so extreme that even the most sensational of the tabloid press would question its veracity.

But I want to believe. And I wonder why?

Why do I wish to imagine the woman I love being subjected to a group sexual attack? Why does the thought of several men using her at once, in every conceivable way, affect me so dramatically? Of course, in these stories she is never in pain or discomfort. In these stories, she reacts positively and enjoys what is happening.

But what she tells me is sometimes so gross I wonder at my mental state to want to hear of it or think of it or pretend I am part of the attack.

Should fantasy stay in the mind or is it possible to physically create your own fantasy? The very thought of considering that course of action is exciting and I know I must go forward. I know I have not yet arrived at the end of this odyssey. Perhaps it will never end. I hope it will never end.

It may change its direction or its meaning but, hopefully, it will never end, for it is not the arrival but the journey that is compelling. Always compelling.

But if I am to bring a fantasy to life, it has to be handled with great care. And such a fantasy must be allowed to develop of its own accord. The circumstances of opportunity must be created and, when they occur, the chances must be taken. Will I be bold enough to take them? Will Gina be bold enough to accept?

I believe she is bold enough, for her experiences have already covered much of the ground I wish to explore. But I wish to explore them from a different direction. In the past she has been a participant, a solo participant, if you like. But I will be a husband watching his wife. And Gina will be a wife indulging in sexual acts while watching her husband watch her and participate himself.

Will she do it? And if she does, will she do it for herself or for me? Will she do it because she wishes to be released from responsibility, because she wants the fullest possible experience of sexual release, because she has the sexual desire, or because I want her to?

Perhaps, like love and lust, the reasons cannot be separated. Such sex as I am contemplating, even now in fantasy, is intoxicating. If I were to fulfil the fantasy with a woman I did not know, a woman I met by chance and for whom I have no love, it would be intoxicating. But to embark upon such sex with my wife as an accomplice makes the intoxication incalculable.

Personally, I find no dichotomy in wanting other men to have sex with my wife, for in my mind I have separated the sex and the love. The love between us is always there. It will always be there. It is that love that gives the sex between us that extra dimension.

But the sex between her and other men – or myself and other women – will not involve love. It will be physical; gloriously, purely physical with no complications of guilt. Any emotion that is released will be based on desire. The love will be mine and Gina's.

I look forward to encountering the opportunities that will enable us both to progress.

Sam finished reading.

'Arabian nights?' she said.

'I did go out with a wealthy Arab once.'

'With bodyguards?'

'No bodyguards, but he had a penchant for attacking from the rear.'

'Drugs and sex and Turkish Delight?'

'When I was a student I smoked dope, like everybody else. It was a phase that I grew out of.'

'Coke?'

'I tried cocaine once. With my Arab. Once was enough.'

'You didn't like it?'

'I liked it too much. It was too dangerous to try twice. I didn't want my nasal passages to collapse or to spend my life on cloud nine. A glass of wine is far more civilised.'

'You sound like a social-worker.'

'You don't do drugs, Sam? Do you?'

'I drink too much gin, but that's legal.'

Gina said, 'I wonder if you can overdose on sex?'

'That could be the final chapter of the book. Is all fair in love and lust? How far should you go for the love of a good man or woman?'

'Don't,' Gina said.

'What's wrong? Am I hitting a little too close to the mark?'

'I don't know. It's as I said before. I feel the journal has taken over. I know it sounds melodramatic, but I don't feel able to stop what is going to happen.'

'You could say no.'

'I couldn't. I've colluded too much. I'm a party to the journal. Hugo asked for tacit approval and I've given it to him.'

'You sound serious.'

Gina forced a smile.

'Perhaps it's my middle-class upbringing. Perhaps it's cold feet.'

'Sodom and Gomorrah were destroyed by brimstone and fire.'

'We have gas central-heating.'

'You'd better check for leaks.'

Gina laughed.

'I don't know what I am worrying about. I haven't had such a good sex life for years, if ever. But it's so good I don't want the bubble to burst.'

Sam put her tongue between her teeth and stared at her friend.

At last she said, 'What about having other men?'

'That's the point. The thought excites me. Sometimes, I'm so randy I could fuck next door's dog.'

'Don't tell Hugo. He might want you to.'

They laughed again.

Gina said, 'Our love life is so good I'm considering going back to work.'

'Sorry?' Sam laughed. 'I don't follow the logic.'

'Neither do I. But it seems to have revitalised me, somehow. Made me aware of life's other possibilities.'

'Gina, if you go on like this, you could turn sex into a born-again religion.'

'It's different for you. You have a career. I gave mine up. I hadn't realised how bored I was.'

'And sex has been the blinding light on the road to Damascus?'

'The road to Harrods food hall maybe.' Gina laughed. 'Don't mock my enthusiasm. I'd forgotten how good sex could be. I'd forgotten how good life could be.'

'It gives a whole new meaning to the story of Sleeping Beauty.'

Gina said, 'You're not taking me seriously.'

'Sorry. There were times when I was rising at seven on a dark November day to go to the office when I quite envied your lifestyle.'

'A lady who lunches? It's like being lobotomised.'

'And sex gave you your brain back?'

Gina grinned.

'It sounds stupid, doesn't it?'

'It sounds like another chapter.' Sam finished the drink and climbed off the stool to fetch more. 'Same again?'

'Of course.'

Gina sat isolated amidst the noise and wondered if logic was playing any part in the games she and Hugo were playing. Had sex really opened her eyes to other aspects of life? At the moment, she and her husband were involved in a shared adventure but how far would they go in pursuit of their fantasies?

Sam returned with two more white-wine spritzers.

'The journal,' she said. 'Will you know when to stop?'

'Of course.'

'Hugo says he wants it to be an odyssey without end. Do you have problems with that?'

'Life is an odyssey.'

'But the journal is structured. Manipulative. We're not talking metaphysics, here.'

'I know that.' Gina smiled. 'We're not talking semantics either. The journal is about sexual excitement and how to maintain it.'

'What about love and marriage?'

'That, too.'

'Gina, are you sure it's not a problem?'

'What?'

'That Hugo may not know when to stop? That he might want to keep going further? That eventually it really will come down to that choice we were talking about – how far do you go for the love of a good man?'

'I think you're overstating it.' Gina was uncomfortable. 'So far, all I've done is tell my husband a few stories and given him an education.'

'Roger Billington?'

'A brief encounter.'

'It was nothing like the film.'

'Sam you're beginning to make me mad.'

'Sorry.'

'Besides, you're still part of this whole thing.'

'I suppose I am.'

'Immortalised in black and white.'

'As I recall, in a script that became progressively more difficult to read.' She gave a cheeky grin. 'I must have been good.'

'You were. Which reminds me. When you come for supper. Hugo suggested we might want to try the kiss again for Brian's benefit.'

'The kiss.' Sam licked her lips. 'It's entered folk lore now, has it? The Kiss?'

'I suppose it has.'

'Supper is beginning to sound like another of your euphemisms for orgy.'

'It isn't and it won't be.' She smiled. 'I have a good feeling about this. Brian will be unable to resist, you'll see. The journal is in control.'

Chapter 23

Supper was informal. It also didn't appear to be leading anywhere. Hugo's high hopes looked as if they would be stillborn.

After lunch in the Sloane Square bar, Gina and Sam had agreed to shelve their reservations. They had enjoyed shopping for silken frivolities and began to look forward to the evening like a school treat at which they planned to misbehave. Nerves showed when the night actually arrived.

Sam wore a black two-piece suit, a silk top in which her breasts moved delightfully, and a heavier split skirt. She wore it with black stockings and high heels, white pearls and with her blonde hair piled upon her head.

Gina had told her she looked stunning when she arrived. Sam had said the outfit was from a chain store. She returned the compliment about Gina's appearance. She wore a cream Jean Muir shift dress in silk jersey.

The talk around the supper table was stilted until they'd had a few glasses of wine. By the time they'd settled themselves after dinner in armchairs and settees, conversation had become more relaxed and intimate.

Hugo said, 'What a terrible job you have, Brian.'
'I like it.'

Brian was as slim and elegant as his wife. He had a permanent tan from his travels.

'But it takes you away too often. From Sam.'

'She's used to it.'

'I don't think I could ever get used to it. Leaving such a beautiful woman every two or three weeks.'

Brian smiled in the direction of his wife, acknowledging of her beauty.

'Unfortunately, it's what I do. It's how I make my living. Don't you ever have to go away?'

'The occasional conference.' Hugo smiled. 'They're bearable only because of the homecoming.'

'Homecoming?'

'Absence, Brian. It makes the heart grow fonder.'

Gina said archly, 'It's not your heart that grows fonder.'

'Hugo grinned at her.

'I've yet to hear you complain, darling.'

'You're getting coarse, Hugo.' She got up and walked across the room. 'Music?'

It was not a question that required a reply. She put a Dire Straits disc in the CD player. The sound was insinuating. A dream beat that wouldn't overpower unless required to.

Gina was aware that Brian had watched her walk across the room. She had purposely chosen to wear the dress without an underslip so that the outline of her underwear would show through according to the movement of her body. As in the story.

The story!

Hugo was watching her now, as Brian averted his gaze. She must remind him to flirt with Sam. Did pompous stuffed shirts know how to flirt?

Gina said, 'Have you never been with Brian on one of his trips, Sam?'

'No.' She crossed her legs and the split skirt parted high on her thigh. 'I've always been busy and, well, the trips are business.'

'You have some free time, don't you, Brian?' Gina said. 'When you're away?'

'Some. Not a lot.'

'What do you do? Sit alone at the bar? Go to nightclubs?'

'I usually have an early night. Sometimes a business dinner. There really isn't that much free time.'

Hugo said, 'I think you're setting yourself too strenuous a pace. You should find time to relax. Seriously. For your health's sake.'

'Seriously?'

Brian smiled at the suggestion.

'When was your last medical check-up?'

'God knows. I'm as fit as a fiddle.'

'You feel good?'

'Yes.'

'Do you get a buzz out of what you do?'

'Yes.'

'The travel, the deals, the success?'

'All of it.'

'The old adrenaline, eh? Keeps you driving on, even after a twelve-hour flight?'

'I like aeroplanes. They don't tire me.'

'When was the last time you had a holiday?'

'I'm always abroad. I don't need a holiday.'

'And Sam?'

'The book fair in Frankfurt. New York, two months ago. They're having a sales conference in Marbella in two months. Do you really think we need holidays?'

'Yes. I do. Away from business. Together.'

Brian's face tightened.

Gina said, 'Stop being medical, Hugo. He means well, Brian, but he does get pompous from time to time. I think he read somewhere that work makes Jack a dull boy. Of course, Jack was probably a miner in Barnsley and never had the chance to travel.'

Sam said, 'I met some miners in Majorca. They weren't dull.'

Hugo grinned and said, 'Sorry, Brian. I suppose I'm basically a homebody. It's as well everybody isn't alike.'

Brian nodded.

'I really am quite fit, Hugo.'

'You certainly look it. But why not call round for a check-up? Everyone should have one at least once a year. No charge.'

Brian laughed.

'No charge? I might take you up on it.'

Sam said, 'What about breast implants?' She moved her right breast with her forearm. 'Would you do those without charge?'

Hugo grinned.

'I've told you before, Sam. You don't need implants. Your breasts are perfect.'

Gina felt a glance cross the room from Brian towards his wife.

'How about a check-up to make sure?' Sam said.

'Anytime you like.'

'Is the bedroom free?' she asked Gina, mischievously.

'Are you trying to make me jealous?' she said.

'Of course not. You can watch if you want.'

Hugo got up and went to the table that held the drinks.

'You sound like schoolgirls, daring each other.'

Sam said, 'We used to be schoolgirls. We used to dare each other.'

Hugo poured himself another brandy.

'What a delightful thought,' he said. 'You two in gym-slips.' He took the bottle to Brian and topped up his drink. 'Can you imagine it?' he asked.

'The way they behave together, yes, I can.'

Sam said, 'St Trinians and stocking tops?' She opened the split of the skirt to display a black ruched garter strap crossing her thigh. 'When we were at school it was bottle green knickers and knee socks.' She closed the skirt.

'Delightful,' said Hugo.

The attention of both he and Brian had been captured by the brief display.

Gina said, 'Actually, we were tomboys at school. Until lights out.'

Brian said, 'Lights out?'

But Gina just laughed and Sam giggled and they allowed alcohol to take the blame for a slip of an indiscretion.

Gina said, 'Who wants to dance?'

Hugo said, 'I'm drinking brandy.'

Brian held up the glass.

'Me, too.'

'I'll dance with you,' said Sam. 'For old times' sake.'

They embraced each other and moved slowly to the gentle beat that now became insidious rather than insinuating. A beat that possibly held seduction.

The men stopped talking. Brian remained sitting in a chair; Hugo was standing by the corridor that led to the kitchen. They watched their wives dance. The bodies of the two women were close together, the material of their dresses hissed against each other, their thighs rubbed. Gina's arms were around Sam's waist; Sam's around Gina's neck.

It was as if the beat had taken them over, that they had forgotten their husbands were in the same room. Their hips moved rhythmically. The music was an excuse but the rhythm was insistent.

Gina felt the tension in the room, in Sam and in herself. They looked into each other's eyes. Gina licked her lips and Sam parted hers. Inexorably, their faces got closer, their lips touched. Once more she could taste Sam's breath. Sam's tongue was the first to invade. They kissed.

The music still played and they still moved to it in a parody of a dance. The kiss was long and deliberate. They ended it when the track ended on the record.

For a moment they remained in each other's arms, a little flustered. Sam's cheeks had a high colour. Hugo applauded. 'So that's what happened after lights out?' he said.

He smiled and his voice was teasing and light-hearted. Exactly right. Gina hadn't thought her husband capable of such subtlety.

'Adolescent girls' stuff,' she said, with a grin, her arm still around Sam's waist as they now faced the two men side by side.

'It was a game,' said Sam. 'We had pin-ups on the wall, photographs of film stars and pop singers, but we never got to kiss a boy.'

Gina said, 'So we kissed each other.'

'And pretended it was a boy. A rock star. Somebody famous.'

'I liked Sting,' Gina said.

'She pretended I was Sting,' Sam said. She shrugged. 'Can you imagine? Me, Sting?'

'You liked Phil Collins.'

'You were about the same height.'

They laughed and Hugo joined in. Brian's smile was unsure but it was a smile.

'Ice,' Hugo said, and went towards the kitchen.

The door closed and Gina said, 'He's forgotten the ice bucket.'

Sam said, 'I'll take it.'

The girls broke apart and Sam took the ice bucket and followed Hugo to the kitchen. Another Dire Straits track had begun. It posed no immediate threat.

'Dance with me, Brian?' Gina said.

His smile had frozen. He was still looking towards the kitchen.

'I don't really dance.'

'You don't really have to. Just move to the music.'

She took the drink from his hand and put it on a coffee table and pulled him to his feet.

'I haven't danced for years,' he said.

'You should. Like Hugo says. Take time off for good behaviour.'

Gina put her arms around his neck and moved close to him. He had no option but to put his arms around her waist. They swayed to the music. He still glanced towards the kitchen but he was not averse to having Gina move as rhythmically as she had with his wife.

She rested her head on his shoulder.

'Music to relax by,' she murmured. 'Wine, a handsome man and a seductive rhythm. What more could you want?'

She nuzzled his neck. 'You smell nice, Brian. What is it?'

'It's . . .' He coughed. 'It's a Calvin Klein.'

'It's nice. Very masculine. Very sexy.'

She could tell his hands were tempted to stray. She could tell he was beginning to become uncomfortable because of the threat of an erection.

Sam had asked her how she felt about having sex with other men and she had replied that the idea appealed to her. Brian appealed to her. Perhaps another time and another place, but only with Sam's approval.

'They're taking a long time?' he said.

'Mmmm?'

Gina moved her hips. The movement was still in time to the music but it was also attuned to his arousal. She felt him stiffening. Her lips went dry and she licked them. It was only a small step in seduction but it made her tingle. His hand slipped surreptitiously over her buttock. It began to follow the strap of her garter belt. His erection became prominent and she could tell he didn't know whether to be blatant about it or pretend it wasn't there.

She sighed deeply and broke the contact. She smiled, kissed him on the cheek and stepped away.

'What are they doing with the ice?' she said, and went down the corridor to the kitchen, leaving Brian standing alone in the middle of the room.

Gina pushed open the door and went into the kitchen. Sam was against the wall, her split skirt open. Hugo was standing between her legs, his hands beneath the skirt and holding her buttocks. They had been kissing but now broke swiftly apart.

They stared at Gina with guilty looks. Gina burst out laughing.

'So much for theory,' she said. 'Passion isn't renewed, it's rampant.'

She walked to them and put her arms around their waists.

'Does he kiss well?' she asked Sam.

'Yes.'

'And have you made his prick stiff?'

Sam was still able to blush.

'Yes.'

'Good. I've done the same for you. Perhaps soon might be the time to go home.'

Sam kissed Gina on the cheek and left the kitchen. Gina moved into her husband's full embrace.

He said, 'You made Brian's prick go stiff?'

'But of course.' She rubbed herself against him. 'How could he resist? Does Sam kiss well?'

'You should know.'

'She does, doesn't she?'

They kissed and his hands pulled up her skirt and touched her flesh. They both shook with urgency but knew it would have to wait. They still had guests.

The kitchen door opened and they looked towards it in surprise. Brian was in the doorway. He looked flustered at seeing Gina with her skirt around her waist, her limbs on show and Hugo's hands upon her bottom.

'Sorry,' he said. 'Sam wanted the ice.'

Gina smiled and pushed down her skirt. Sam would. Sam knew exactly the situation that Brian would walk into. She picked up the full ice bucket.

'Coming now,' she said, and heard Hugo sigh.

They went back to the music and the drinks but the moment was in abeyance. Sam and Gina flirted with each other, and Brian could not stop looking at his wife's legs where the split kept getting wider.

It was not long before Sam yawned and blinked through too much wine. She had read the journal, Gina thought, she knew how it was done.

They left, politely and obeying social conventions. Gina wondered how long the conventions would last in the bedroom when Sam needed undressing.

Chapter 24

Gina resisted the urge to telephone Sam the next day to find out what had happened. Her resolve was wearing thin by the day after when Sam eventually called.

'Well?' said Gina.

Sam laughed. She sounded like a disembodied ghost.

'Very well, thank you.'

'It worked?'

'You want the details?'

'Of course I want the details.'

'I didn't come into the office yesterday. I stayed in bed.'

'All day?'

'It's been a long time.'

Gina was delighted for her friend.

'Was it good?'

'It was amazing. When he flagged, I even told him a story.'

'Did it work?'

'Of course it worked. It was one of your stories.'

'I'm so pleased, Sam.'

'So am I. Have you had any more adventures?'

'Not adventures. But Hugo was a bit eager after you went. You really did get him going for me.'

'He's a handsome man.'

'So is Brian.'

There was a pause as they both thought about the direction the conversation was going.

Gina said, 'I could very easily make love to Brian, Sam, but I don't think it would be a good idea.'

'What's all this making love, all of a sudden? What happened to fucking?'

Sam articulated the word down the telephone line. It was as if she had touched Gina with a live electric wire.

'Okay. I could fuck him.' She articulated back. 'But I don't think it would be a good idea.'

'I know what you mean. I could fuck Hugo, too. But that's playing a little close to home, isn't it?'

Gina laughed. Sexual tension was once more alive and well in a conversation that had started almost normally.

'Listen to us,' she said. 'A few weeks ago, we were locked into our marriages as if we were locked into prison cells. Bound with chastity belts. Now we're talking about fucking other men over the telephone.'

'Now there's a concept . . .'

'Sam!'

'I always wondered about telephone sex. I thought perhaps they used special receivers. I think the one I'm using would be distinctly uncomfortable.'

'Be serious, for a moment.'

'Do I have to?'

'Yes. I think the journal has taken us close enough. I don't think we should tempt fate by letting it take us closer.'

'You mean as in swopping?'

'That's a terrible expression but, yes, that's what I mean.'

'I've just got Brian back. I don't want to swop.'

'I'm talking of the future, Sam.'

'Sounds like you've thought about this?'

'I have. I did. The other night when I was dancing with Brian. I thought how easy it would be to go to bed with him. How I would enjoy it. I even told myself that if I did, it would have to be with your permission.'

'Thank you.'

Gina couldn't tell whether Sam was being flippant or sarcastic.

'I've thought about it,' she said. 'We've talked about it. The momentum? I think that's the danger. You create the right set of circumstances, as Hugo likes to say, and things happen. If they happened between the four of us, I think it could be a mistake.'

'That's not part of Hugo's plan, is it?'

'No. Of course not.'

'Of course not? You sound as if your worries are specific.'

'They're not. It's just that things can get out of hand and it's best not for them to get out of hand between friends.'

'What about what happened between us?'

'That was different. We're no threat to each other's marriages.'

'And sex between strangers is okay?'

'Much safer if you want to protect your relationship.'

Sam didn't say anything for a moment.

'I think maybe you're taking things too seriously again. Gina. All Hugo and I did was kiss.'

'I know that. I'm thinking of some time in the future. Some other supper party. Some . . .'

'Some time that may never come.'

'Some time when the novelty of sex with your husband has

worn off and you don't want to lose the excitement. Some time when you might be tempted to go one step further.'

'Who are you talking about, Gina? You or me?'

Gina had started making her points with a clarity of purpose. Friends who saw each other regularly, knew each other, were more likely to become emotionally involved with each other if they had sexual affairs. That was logical. Sex with strangers was preferable.

At least, the points had seemed to be clear in her mind when she had started. Now she was no longer sure.

'I am, aren't I?' she said. 'Talking about me?'

'You can always say no, Gina.'

'I can't.'

'The momentum?'

'Yes. I can't stop it. Not yet.'

'When?'

'I'll know when.'

Sam said, 'You know, getting Brian back, it's sort of broken the obsession for me. With the journal.'

'Obsession? Is it an obsession?'

'I think so. I could feel it. I felt it when you came round. The kiss? I was being carried along, too. You said I was a participant and I was. If it hadn't worked with Brian, I'd probably be joining you in the next fantasy. Three in a bed with Hugo? But I broke it.'

'I thought you liked the journal?'

'I did. I still do. But I've become an observer.' She laughed to lighten the tension between them. 'I've retreated into my profession. I've become objective, an editor.'

Gina wondered if Sam was right.

'Am I obsessed with sex, Sam?'

'That was just an expression. I overstated the case.'

'I wonder.'

'It's good, isn't it? You're still enjoying it?'

'Of course I am. We both are.'

'Then who am I to criticise. What two consenting adults get up to, is their business.' Sam laughed. 'You were always too serious, Gina. You'd analyse an egg boiling.'

'Maybe I should have done the psychology course.'

'Maybe you're doing it now. Look, how about lunch on Friday? We can talk properly.'

'Can't. We're going away for the weekend.'

'Where?'

'Somerset.'

'Why?'

'Change of scenery. Get away from London and all its chaos.'

'Looking for new opportunities?'

'Maybe that as well.'

'Why Somerset?'

'Hugo knows the area. He has friends down there.'

'Watch out for friends bearing gifts of cider.'

'Are you writing the script?'

'I wouldn't dare. Hugo does it so much better.'

Gina couldn't quite tell if there was an implied criticism in the way Sam made the remark.

'Look, Sam, you know I talked about betting back into PR? I've thought further about taking some part-time freelance work. Would there be anything in your publicity department?'

'Are you serious?'

'Of course.' She laughed. 'I told you, all this sex has activated my brain cells as well as my little monster.' They both laughed. 'I want to become a working girl, again.'

'Well, I'll ask, but I don't know if we'll have anything. If you like, I'll spread the word around. Let it be known you're available.'

'Thanks, Sam. I'll make some calls next week when I get back.'

'Is this an attempt to slow down the momentum?'

'I don't think so. If I'm honest, I like the momentum. I like the danger, too. The unknown. If I'm honest, I like fucking. The scary part is, I don't know how much.'

'So all this talk . . .?'

'Is talk. Ideas in your head are one thing, putting them into words lets you inspect them. They suddenly look different, sound different, feel different.' She laughed. 'It's like squeezing spots.'

'What a delightful simile.'

'That's all psychology is, isn't it? Squeezing spots?'

'I'm glad I didn't make it a career choice.'

They laughed and made arrangements to get in touch the following week.

Gina felt better when she put down the receiver. The doubts were impurities in her mind. telling Sam was one way of getting rid of them. It was true, she did enjoy the momentum, and she did enjoy fucking. The only doubt was how much. When it came to making fantasy real, would she enjoy it more than her husband?

Chapter 25

They escaped London in the middle of Friday afternoon.
Hugo drove the BMW along the M4 towards Bristol. Gina
had never been to Somerset before. He told her it was a
county of stunning beauty. He also said he had an old friend
who still lived there whom he had arranged to meet.

'You'll like Philip. We were medical students together
but he never finished. He gave it up. He always wanted to
be a writer.'

'Did he become one?'

'Eventually. He became a school-teacher first.'

'Sam says there's no money in writing. Unless you're
Jeffrey Archer.'

'Philip isn't Jeffrey Archer but he makes a living.'

'What does he write?'

'Historical romance. He's surrounded by wind-swept
moors and fishing villages. It's a very romantic place.'

'Where are we staying?'

'Somewhere romantic.'

Gina wondered of Hugo's friend would figure in any of
their weekend activities but decided it was wrong to antici-
pate. Whatever happened, would happen.

The journey was made tiresome by traffic, particularly

when they left the M5 to take the narrow coastal road from Bridgewater. But Hugo had not exaggerated. The villages they went through were pretty, the pubs inviting and the sea and the hills of the Quantocks and Exmoor proved a captivating combination.

No wonder Hugo's writer friend lived here. It was a landscape made for romantic fiction. Perhaps a landscape where fantasies came true.

As they approached Minehead, Gina's breath was taken away by the beauty of a castle that rose tall from a hillside forest across a meadow.

'Dunster Castle,' Hugo announced, as if he had performed a trick. He turned along a road signposted to Dunster village.

'It's absolutely perfect,' said Gina.

'Wait till you see the village.'

Dunster was a fitting adjunct to the fairy-tale castle – a medieval village with cobbled streets and latticed windows, courtyards and alleyways.

He parked the car at the Dunster Castle Hotel.

'What do you think?' he said.

'It's marvellous.'

Their romance continued over dinner of duck paté and Exmoor trout and chablis and, later still, in their room with chilled champagne and relaxed love-making.

Gina forgot she had ever had doubts.

Rain had cleansed the cobbles by morning but the clouds broke as they had breakfast.

'You've arranged everything,' she said, as the sun splashed onto the main street.

'I hope so,' he said.

He wore blue slacks and a yellow cashmere sweater that she had bought him. Gina wore flat shoes and ankle socks and short blue dress of jersey cotton. Hugo complimented her appearance.

'You look so young, I feel like your father,' he said.

'Are you complaining?'

'Not at all. But I may not be able to keep my hands off you.'

'That's the idea.'

They explored the village, the Chantry of St Lawrence, the Priory Church, the shops, potteries and galleries. Hugo remained attentive, touching her at every opportunity. Perhaps he was obsessive, too, she thought. There were worse things to be obsessive about than each other.

Late in the morning, they drove out of Dunster and back along the coast road before turning off at the village of Kilve.

'That must be it,' he said.

The house was a white-walled cottage with roses round the door. Hugo parked in a lane at the side and as they got out of the car, a man came out to greet them.

Philip was about Hugo's age, slim but smaller. His build was athletic and he moved neatly. He wore blue jeans and a blue denim shirt, a lot of dark hair and small gold stud in his right ear. He grinned with even white teeth as he shook her hand.

'Hugo did not exaggerate,' he said. 'You are very beautiful.'

She laughed and they went into the cottage through the back door. The smell of percolating coffee filled the house and he showed them into the living room before returning to the kitchen to pour it into three mugs.

The cottage was deceptive. The living room was large with an inglenook fireplace and two expansive settees with soft cushions. Thick goatskin rugs littered the floor. The walls were lined with full bookshelves. A chess set that featured the opposing armies of Wellington and Napoleon had its own table in a corner. They had come through the kitchen and past a dining room on a level two steps down.

Philip came in carrying a tray with the coffee.

'From outside, this place looks so small,' Gina said. 'Yet there's so much space.'

'I'll show you round, if you like.'

Leading off the dining room was his study, lined with more books. A word processor sat on a desk, piles of paper and books on another.

Hugo said, 'This is where you sit and wait for inspiration, is it?'

'No such thing. You sit and start writing. It's the only way. At least it's the only way I can do it.'

Gina said, 'It seems to have been successful.'

He grinned.

'It keeps the bailiff from the door and it's better than working.'

Gina said, 'My friend is in publishing. I know it's hard work.'

'But it doesn't seem like hard work. Not if you don't mind the solitude.'

'Is solitude an essential part of being a writer?' Gina asked.

'It's essential to be able to live inside your own brain,' he said. 'But the solitude – at least, my solitude – gets in the way of relationships. I tried twice and failed both times. My partners couldn't get used to sharing me with the characters in my head.'

Gina smiled.

'So you prefer fantasy to relationships?'

'I don't prefer. That's the way it is.'

Hugo said, 'It seems strange that a writer of romance can't organise his own love life.'

'I haven't been totally without female companionship,' Philip said. 'There are one or two ladies I see from time to time.'

'Mutual need?' Hugo said.

'Something like that.'

They went back into the dining room. A square staircase divided it from the kitchen. He pointed upwards.

'Three bedrooms and inside plumbing.'

Hugo said, 'You say that as if inside plumbing is unusual in the country.'

'Visitors from London sometimes think it is.'

Gina said, 'Not these visitors. Your cottage is lovely.'

'I think so. Four hundred years old and walls that breathe stories.'

'Breathe stories?' said Gina.

'I think they whisper plots to me when I'm asleep.'

'What a delightful notion,' she said. 'Are they always romance?'

'Not always.'

After coffee, he suggested he be their guide and they readily agreed. Gina insisted on sitting in the back of the car so Philip could have the passenger seat and direct Hugo. She sat behind her husband, her legs crossed, conscious of the length of tanned thigh the short skirt displayed.

Philip sat sideways to be able to speak to both of them.

She knew he was conscious of her thighs as well.

He was a good-looking man and he was a stranger. Someone they could drive away from and leave in the depths of the country when the weekend was over. It was up to Hugo to indicate what should happen. Already, she could feel the tension between her and her husband. Perhaps that would be enough.

Or perhaps he would not want the fantasy consummated?

Gina licked her lips and pressed her thighs together. She did.

Philip took them to Nether Stowey, the village where Coleridge lived when he wrote The Rime of the Ancient Mariner.

They looked round the small cottage the poet had lived in. Two rooms on the ground floor were open, filled with his furniture and books. There were busts of him upon tables and portraits upon the walls.

Dust motes danced and the air was musty. They were the only visitors. The only sound, apart from squeaking floor-boards, was the tick of a grandfather clock. An elderly attendant remained in the hallway by the stairs at a table that sold mementos and publications.

'He was brilliant,' Philip said. 'Although his genius may have been prompted in his younger days. He enjoyed opium. Read him and you drown in his imagery.'

'I've read him,' said Gina. 'But a long time ago.'

Philip excused himself and went into the hall to talk to the attendant. Gina was facing a window onto the street. Across the road was The Ancient Mariner public house. Hugo moved close behind her. His hands held her hips and he pushed himself against her. She could feel him big in his trousers.

'Poets and history,' he whispered in her ear. 'Less than inspiring.'

She pushed herself back against him.

'This poet was inspired. He wallowed in fantasy.'

Hugo's erection was upright and lay between her buttocks. He moved his hips against hers, rubbing it in the soft valley. She glanced sideways at a painting of the poet's cherubic face as a young man. From the hallway, they could hear Philip still talking to the attendant.

They were alone, the ticking of the clock a metronome of timelessness. Alone but for the images of Coleridge upon the walls and tables and mantelpiece, who watched them without judgement, but with that slight, knowing smile upon his lips.

Hugo slid the dress upwards and she did not stop him. He bunched it around her waist and his hands were on her flesh, feeling her buttocks, holding her hips and pulling her against him. His breath was measured against her neck.

'I could fuck you now,' he whispered.

'Yes.'

'Would you let me?'

'Yes.'

His right hand moved around her body and over her abdomen. His fingers pushed beneath her panties and stroked her vagina. The lips of her sex opened and his finger slid into the silky wetness. She leaned her head against his shoulder and groaned. She was on the verge of orgasm already.

The conversation in the hallway stopped. Hugo removed his fingers and held her by both hips, her skirt still raised at the back. He turned her to face the doorway, his erection still pressing against her.

Philip looked into the room. His smile was like that of the poet. Slight, knowing, without judgement. He held a book which he raised in one hand to show them.

'I bought you a present,' he said to Gina.

Hugo finally removed his hands and she moved half a pace forward and the skirt dropped down behind her.

'We must find something to give you,' Hugo said to Philip.

They drove next to Combe Sydenham, through the Quantock Forest and into the Brendon Hills. On the journey, Gina admired the book Philip had bought her: an illustrated edition of the Ancient Mariner. Philip admired her tanned thighs in the short dress.

Combe Sydenham was a small country park in which stood a Tudor manor house. They paid an entrance fee and entered the grounds. Birds sang and the sun was hot. Peacocks strutted along a high wall.

'This is enchanting,' Gina said.

'So is the legend,' said Philip.

'What legend?'

They went through a gateway and walked towards the manor house.

'The lady of the house, Elizabeth Sydenham, was engaged to be married to Sir Francis Drake. But he was away at sea for longer than expected, and she was courted by someone else. She agreed to marry this new gentleman and was on her way to church for the wedding when there was a flash, a bang and a cannonball hurtled out of the sky and fell at her feet.'

Gina laughed.

'A cannonball?' she said.

'It was supposed to have been fired by Drake and

travelled halfway around the world. Whatever it was, Elizabeth got the message. She turned around and went home and cancelled the wedding. She waited for Drake and, when he got back, they were married.'

Hugo said, 'What an amazing story.'

'Was there any truth in it?' said Gina.

'There must be. They still have the cannonball in the hall. If you touch it, it is supposed to bring you luck.'

'A real cannonball?' said Gina.

'It has been suggested it was a meteorite that fell at Lady Elizabeth's feet.'

They entered the hall. It was still in a state of restoration although the ceiling had been repainted in glorious detail and colour. A middle-aged lady in twin set and pearls and sensible brogues was on duty. Drake's cannonball sat in the fireplace upon a wooden cradle. Gina crouched before it and stroked its black and pitted surface.

'For luck?' she said, glancing at Hugo.

'For luck.'

'Should I make a wish as well?'

He chuckled.

'Why not?'

Philip was talking to the woman attendant. Gina got the impression he knew her slightly, perhaps from visiting the hall on a regular basis to maintain good fortune in publishing, if not in his love life. In the corner of the room was a rough wooden ladder.

'May I?' Gina said to the woman.

'Of course. But be careful.'

The woman and Philip continued to talk. Gina climbed the ladder and Hugo followed behind. At the top, they entered a small room from where they could look over the grounds from a window or peep back down into the hall.

Gina faced the window and Hugo, without preliminaries, pulled up her dress to her waist. She gasped. She had expected to be touched but not to be attacked. She reached out and placed a hand on either side of the stone window-frame.

He was not interested in kissing or in romance. He wanted swift sex without trammels. He pushed her panties down around her thighs and his hands gripped her buttocks and went between her legs and touched her.

She had not realised how highly aroused she had been. The tension had been latent, waiting only for a touch or the circumstance to be released. His fingers went into her and she pushed herself onto them. Her body was shaking, muscles quivering and her breath was ragged.

Hugo unzipped his trousers. She heard the sound but did not believe it was happening. Not Hugo, not there. But his penis, hot and hard, was between her legs, the head nudging between the lips of her sex.

No, she thought. Not here. We can't. Not here.

But her body was demanding the opposite. It wanted penetration, satisfaction. It wanted an end to the shaking of her limbs, an end to the sexual palsy that she knew could only be relieved by orgasm.

Gina braced herself, parting her legs as far the panties would allow, and Hugo held apart her opening and pushed his penis inside.

Oh my God, oh my God . . .

The last time she had heard those words had been when she had virtually raped Sam in her apartment. She had pushed her against the wall and taken her. Now her husband was doing the same to her and she felt her tensions breaking so much that she did not know if she could remain standing for very much longer.

He gripped her hips and thrust violently, desperately. Below them, she could hear the well-modulated voice of the lady attendant. So well-modulated, she could actually be the lady of the house. Up here, in this tiny room, the only sounds were Hugo's gasps and her own breath and that keened from her throat.

Hugo yelped and buried his face in her neck. His fingers gripped her hips tighter and he came. His thighs shuddered and his penis discharged inside her.

Her eyes were open but had been sightless as they stared out of the window. Now she saw the blue sky, the green trees and heard the noises of the birds outside, and the voice of the lady of the house down below. Gina experienced where she was in time, place and sex with startling clarity.

She had once more become sex. Her husband had been unable to resist her. Philip down below wanted her. She felt capable of seducing anyone. Perhaps even the middle-aged lady of the house.

It was as if sex was a palpable force, a ley line of ancient power into which she had tapped. She had not climaxed, but the perception was more important. Her husband sagged behind her, a mere man without the stamina or insight of a woman. His limp penis slipped from her and he hastily fastened his clothing.

Gina gloried in the wetness between her legs. She remained, hands on either side of the window, staring out at her world where all things were possible. Behind her, Hugo pulled her panties back into place and her skirt dropped to respectability.

'We should go down,' he murmured.

He went down first and she followed.

The lady looked at them quizzically.

'Not a lot to see up there,' she said.

'We were enjoying the view,' said Hugo, his face flushed.

Gina said nothing. She smiled at the woman and went back to the fireplace and crouched by Drake's cannonball.

Philip came to her side.

'Ready?' he said.

She stroked the blackened ball.

'Just one more wish,' she said.

Chapter 26

They went to a village pub in Stogumber and ate a late lunch. Gina drank wine. The weather changed and black clouds rolled in turning the summer afternoon dark. A thunderclap sounded.

Gina said, 'Another cannon shot from Drake?'

'A warning?' Philip said.

'I'm already married,' she said.

Was it a warning?

Rain poured down and the skies got blacker. When it eased, they ran to the car and Hugo drove back to Kilve.

Philip said, 'I apologise for the weather, but this part of Somerset has a reputation for rain.'

'This isn't rain,' said Hugo. 'It's a deluge.'

He parked in the lane and Philip dashed to unlock the back door of the cottage. Hugo ran for cover but Gina was in no rush. She stood in the garden and stared at the dark, stormy sky. More thunder clapped and lightning flashed in jagged anger.

Hugo shouted from the cottage.

'You're getting soaked.'

She smiled at the storm and at the sky and felt her dress clinging to her body. Of course she was getting soaked. It felt good, like a baptism. An immersion.

Gina at last went into the cottage. Coffee was percolating again, a wonderful evocative smell, but she did not want coffee.

Hugo said, 'You're wet through, darling.'

Philip said, 'A hot drink?'

'I'd rather have a brandy.'

Their host pointed into the living room.

'In there. I've lit the fire. How about you, Hugo?'

'I'll have brandy, too.'

The sixteenth century cottage had a gas fire. She hadn't taken much notice earlier, but what she had imagined to be logs and coal in the inglenook fireplace were the facia of an instant gas fire.

Nothing was ever as it seemed, she thought, and stopped herself from bursting into laughter.

Philip followed them with a brandy bottle and glasses. He poured drinks and she sipped hers greedily, feeling the false heat entering her body, aware of the way the silk jersey clung to her curves.

'You can't stay in those,' Philip said. 'I'll find you something. You, too, Hugo. We're all wet through.'

He went upstairs. She looked at her husband. Rain still trickled down her face. He put his arms around her and kissed her gently. His trousers denied his gentleness. They held his stiffness again. He had recovered his desire.

Gina opened her mouth and kissed him properly. Her tongue demanded attention. His penis stiffened against her belly; his hands gripped her buttocks.

Philip coughed from the doorway. He had taken off his clothes and wore a blue towelling robe. His legs were brown.

'I've put some stuff out on the bed,' he said. 'Some of it belongs to an old girlfriend. I hope you don't mind.'

She smiled at him, stepped away from her husband and went upstairs.

'Back bedroom,' he shouted, from below. 'Put your wet things over the radiators. I've put the heating on.'

A white towelling robe lay on the bed along with a variety of other garments, some female, some male. Gina stripped off the dress, panties, socks and shoes. She chose an item from the selection and took it to the bathroom. She walked along the corridor and smiled as her husband reached the top of the stairs.

He stopped her, excited by her nakedness, and touched her but she prevented his kisses.

'Later,' she said, ambiguously.

She went into the bathroom and closed the door.

When she went downstairs, Hugo was there. He wore the white towelling robe.

'How do I look?' she said.

Gina wore a white cotton dress with a halter neck. Her nipples showed through the material and the skirt of the dress was short and full. She wore no panties.

Philip said, 'You look like a milkmaid.'

She displayed her empty brandy glass and he got up and refilled it. The room was already muggy. The atmosphere appealed to her. It was heavy with moisture and heat. The rain continued to pour and the skies were so dark that Philip had lit a lamp in the corner of the room.

'Draw the curtains,' she said. It was neither a request nor an order but she knew she would be obeyed. 'When it storms outside, we should be cosy inside.'

Philip drew the curtains and the room became darker, lit

only by the distant lamp and the glow of the false fire. He put on music. Eric Clapton played relaxed guitar.

'I'm sorry about the weather,' he said.

She sat in a corner of a settee, Hugo in the other corner. Philip sprawled on the other settee, which was at right angles. He leaned over and took something from a bookshelf.

'Do you smoke?' he said.

'No,' said Hugo.

'Smoke what?' said Gina.

'Dope.'

She smiled.

'What a lovely idea.'

Hugo glanced at her but said nothing. He sipped the brandy and they watched Philip go through the ritual of rolling a joint. Always rituals, Gina thought. Rituals in everything.

He lit the cigarette, inhaled and held the smoke. He inhaled again and passed the cigarette to Gina. It had been a long time since she had smoked. She took a deep drag and waited for the burn. Inhaled again and passed it to Hugo. He followed her example.

They sat around without talking, drinking brandy and smoking. It was another of those times when words were unnecessary. So often, words got in the way. Made false promises, built barricades, destroyed moments. But now, they did not speak. They smiled and the tension in the room changed to expectation.

Gina wondered how it would start. She could start it herself but she felt too much in control. Hugo should start it. If he sensed her control, he might be worried.

Philip had put a stack of discs on the CD player and the

music changed but was always mellow and had a pleasant beat that corresponded with the pulse of her vagina. He sat on the floor, so as to be able to pass the joints easier, but now they had stopped smoking. She stood up and reached past him for the brandy bottle.

Hugo got off the settee and stood close to her. She turned into his arms and smiled at him. He took the bottle and glass from her and handed them to Philip. He put his arms around her and kissed her. Their mouths opened and they tasted each other's lust.

Her body melted against his and, as always, she felt his erection. His hands went beneath the short milkmaid skirt and onto her bottom. Behind her, Philip remained on the floor, watching. She reached between her and Hugo and opened the robe and found his penis. The kiss broke and he licked her face.

'Fuck me,' she whispered.

His penis shuddered. His hands moved over her back and he unfastened the straps of the dress behind her neck. The bodice fell loose from her breasts. The dress remained fastened at her waist and he fumbled to find the fastening. She reached behind her and unbuttoned it and the dress fell from her and pooled at her feet.

Hugo shrugged the robe from his shoulders and it fell from him. They embraced in their nakedness, their flesh hot and wanting. Their hands tentatively demanding, for they both knew there was a long way to go.

He turned her and held her against him so that his penis lay between the soft globes of her buttocks. Philip still sat at her feet, staring up her body and into her face that now felt heavy. So heavy, she could no longer smile. All she wanted was sex, not smiles.

Her husband reached around her to hold her breasts, to grip them in his palms and rub the nipples with his thumbs. She leaned her head back against his shoulder and felt him move his erection against her, a smooth, slow, friction that lubricated itself. Her lips parted and she groaned and closed her eyes.

The sex was ethereal, the sensations muted by heat and cannabis and brandy, until Philip put his mouth to her vagina. The contact was both natural and unexpected. She moaned loudly and squirmed in her husband's arms as if seeking escape, but he held her.

Oh my God, oh my God . . .

Philip parted the swollen lips of her vagina and his mouth was greedy on the flesh within. He licked and sucked and she was lost, no longer in control, but a victim once more, always a victim, and the orgasm that had been waiting all day swept forward powerfully and took her on its crest.

Gina wondered what the noise was and realised it was her. The climax had passed and left her whimpering in her husband's arms. She was being moved, laid down upon a settee, and her legs were being positioned.

She opened her eyes and saw Hugo above her. He was entering her, kneeling between her legs and pushing his penis into her. She arched her back to make the entry easier and groaned loudly as he went inside.

'Fuck me,' she whispered.

Hugo fucked her forcefully until he had expended his initial lust, and then more slowly, not wanting to finish too soon. He was panting and sweating, his face that of a stranger. Sex made everybody strangers, she thought.

Philip was kneeling by the settee watching their congress. She reached down and found his penis. Hot and stiff, pounding with blood. Romance had gone from his expression. Only lustful fantasy remained. She leaned her face sideways and licked her lips. She opened her mouth and made it a vagina.

Her husband realised what she was doing and groaned and held himself rigid inside her. He looked at the writer and gulped. Both men licked their lips for saliva.

'Do it,' Hugo hissed.

Philip knelt up and his penis was level with Gina's face. She stroked it, held it above her lips, and stared past it, up into the eyes of her husband and remembered another time, in the back of a car. Her tongue slid out and she licked the penis delicately and still her husband held himself without movement, deeply embedded inside her.

Gina turned her head, manoeuvred Philip's erection, and slowly slid the head of the glans into her mouth. She held it there, mouth tightly clamped around it, holding it between thumb and forefinger around its base, aware of her husband's stare. She salivated in her throat and her cheeks sank in and then extended out and she began to suction the penis in her mouth.

Hugo grunted and shuddered but did not come. He still held himself in check. She sucked with abandon, moving her head so that the glans bulged her cheek, taking it from her mouth to lick the eye with her lascivious tongue, rubbing the end across her face.

Her husband gave in and began to thrust into her once more, fiercely and with passion, and all the time he stared into her face as she sucked another man's penis. She had expected him to come quickly but he didn't and she raised her thighs and wrapped her feet around his back as his assault slapped against her.

Her fingers worked swiftly at the base of Philip's penis and he gasped at the wantonness of her caress. He raised himself from his knees to lean over her and he gave a strangled cry and came, his penis jumping as it discharged its juice.

He finished, gasped and fell away onto the floor and Gina stared into her husband's face and opened her mouth to show him that the sperm was still there, white pools of another man's fluid upon her tongue and on her teeth.

Now Hugo could not stop himself. His eyes bulged and, as he came, his mouth covered hers and their tongues divided the spoils.

The three of them lay in stupor for a while until Hugo climbed from her and leaned against a bookcase to pour more brandy. Philip staggered from the room, as if he could still not believe what had happened. He returned with an open bottle of champagne.

They mixed the brandy and the champagne, Philip sprawled once more on the other settee, her husband standing by the fireplace, the glow of the false coals colouring his body shades of bronze and red, the shadows deep at his front around his genitals.

Gina knew this was only a temporary break but she couldn't wait. She lay on her back and stared at their shadowed faces and she put her hands between her legs and began to play with her little beast.

At first, she wanted to watch their reaction but soon she became lost in the delights that her fingers were releasing. Her eyes closed, her head tilted back and her hips moved. Three fingers of her left hand were inside herself, making noises as they plunged rhythmically. Two fingers of her right hand delicately worked the rosebud.

Her thigh muscles began to tense and clamp around her hands and she gasped, almost in surprise, and came, shaking upon the settee, lying upon another stage, before another audience.

Her performance banished the lethargy of her lovers and the men – for in her mind they had now become men rather than Hugo and Philip – began a new assault upon her.

Now she sucked one while the other took her from the rear, all three lying on the broad cushions of the settee. Now she knelt upon the floor as they changed the permutation. Now she was bent over the arm of the furniture. Now she had two pricks presented to her and licked them both and rubbed them in her face and her hair.

Now her husband sodomised her and made her scream because she had not thought anything else could penetrate the sexual haze in which she was lost. He pierced her to the soul and she welcomed it. He rolled sideways among the goatskin rugs of the floor, and she lay pinned upon him, her limbs spreadeagled.

Her other lover hesitated at her front, his penis held against the portals of her vagina. He licked her neck, her face. His fingers entered her but not his prick.

'Do it!' she hissed.

He pushed and it went inside. He pushed again and the whole length penetrated her and she was pinioned and totally beyond safety. She gave herself up to the sex and the orgasm and, for a while, she lost her mind.

Chapter 27

Hugo did not write in the journal for four days after they got back from the weekend in Somerset. They were both shell-shocked, she supposed. She didn't even want to see Sam. Before she could talk about what happened, she had to allow the incident to gain a perspective. She also had to fit it into the context of her husband's perceptions.

They had sex every night. But swift and silent sex, without talk. He ensured she orgasmed at least twice on each occasion before he climaxed. But they didn't talk.

The morning she found the journal on the desk waiting for her after he had gone to his clinic, she left it there for an hour before she dared look. She took it to the bedroom and lay upon the bed. She opened the book and found a new entry but kept her eyes unfocused. She took a deep breath and she allowed the words to make sense. She began to read:

I have been in a quandary since our return, not knowing how to describe my emotions. It occurred to me to be circumspect in order to save my own feelings as well as those of Gina, but I can only be honest. What happened that weekend was absolutely incredible.

It was a culmination of a dream and I discovered that the reality was better. To watch Gina in the wildness of abandonment made me love her all the more. What a wonderful creature she is! What a beautiful passionate woman! How lucky I am to possess her.

Possession. That was the key to my sanity during that wonderful experience. For she belonged to me and I to her. We belong to each other and to no-one else. Anyone else is simply a prick to be fucked or sucked. The emotions are ours. The love is ours.

Because of this, when I recount what happened I will not use the name of the third party. He was the guest at our feast and he will remain anonymous. For the same reason, at this moment, I never want to see him again.

This decision has not been made of jealousy or guilt or shame. The reason is so that I am better able to isolate this incident from the mundane, to keep it, if you like, as fantasy.

But the memories of that day, that whole day, are so vivid and so marvellous. Even after only these few paragraphs, my penis is engorged. I do not know if we can ever recapture the intensity of that occasion but I look forward to the circumstances presenting themselves where other opportunities may arise.

And now, I shall endeavour to tell the story of our day in the country.

Her husband went into greater detail than ever before and covered page after page with feelings, descriptions and obscenities as he catalogued all that they had done.

Gina's cheeks suffused and her senses bubbled and she touched herself as she read and, before she finished the entry, she had brought herself to three rolling climaxes that had followed each other like breakers on a wide beach.

His feelings matched hers. She was reassured. The journal was still open for business. There were more adventures ahead. Years before, she had known when to stop the cycle of events with Billy and her cousin in the car. But this was different. This was two consenting adults and she had never felt so full of sex in her life before.

What next?

That depended upon the right set of circumstances.

They occurred two days later. Hugo was to attend a conference in Newcastle and invited her to go with him. They left in the car in the evening and took the M1 to Leeds where they checked into a modern city-centre hotel.

The room was large and comfortable and nondescript and she showered first and came out of the bathroom in black underwear and stockings and high heels.

'You could tempt the devil like that,' he said.

Her reflection in the full length mirror made her believe he was not exaggerating. The stockings were sleek with a high sheen, the garter straps taut, the panties high cut and the bra low cut. Her breasts appeared to be in danger of falling from the cups.

'Take a good look,' she said. 'It's going away until later.'

She stepped into a black shift dress, zipped it and smoothed it over her hips. It followed her contours delightfully and showed her cleavage.

'You look good enough to buy,' he said.

'That's a strange thing to say.' She smiled. Her Coleridge smile. 'Why don't you?'

'What do you mean?'

'I'm going down now. When you come down, why don't you proposition me? See if I'm for sale?'

He laughed but she saw the colour high in his cheeks and knew she had hit the right spot with the suggestion. While he watched, she slipped the wedding ring from her finger and put it in her handbag.

The lift took her to the foyer. The hotel had a ballroom, conference rooms and several bars. A convention was being held for financial consultants. Gina chose the quietest bar, away from the noise of the convention guests. She sat on a circular bench seat in an alcove behind a low table. A potted plant to the right made it semi-private.

A waiter brought her a large gin and tonic. She relaxed, her legs crossed high, and she surveyed the rest of the patrons. They were less than inspiring.

Two men in their twenties came in and sat at the bar. They also surveyed the room and saw her. They exchanged looks between each other and a whispered conversation ensued. She smiled to herself. She might get an offer before Hugo got here.

The taller of the men left the bar and came across the room. He walked self-consciously. He could have been making the approach as a bet. He was in his mid-twenties. He wore a suit, shirt and tie, and was halfway to present-able with blond hair. She guessed he was part of the convention.

'Are you on your own?' he said.

'I'm waiting for someone.'

'It's not me, is it?'

He grinned and swayed from the hips. Body language to his friend. I'm in and pitching.

'I don't think so.'

'Ah! So there's a possibility?'

Gina smiled. A private smile, and looked him slowly up and down.

'I don't think you could afford me,' she said.

A quick blush touched his face and he licked his bottom lip. She immediately felt sorry that she had upset his feelings. He retaliated with bluster.

'That depends how much you charge.'

Gina maintained the smile.

'You'd better ask the gentleman who's just walked in. He's paying.'

The young man turned and saw Hugo coming towards them. He glanced back at Gina and gave her a nod that could have meant goodbye or, perhaps, I'll ask him. He went back to the bar and as he passed Hugo, he nodded again but did not speak.

Hugo sat down.

'Who was that?'

'An admirer. He wants to know how much I would cost.'

'Did you tell him?'

'I said he should ask you. You were paying.'

He raised his eyebrows and smiled.

'So how much am I paying?'

'How much am I worth? What is the going rate for a hooker?'

'One like you?' He shrugged. 'Ones like you only happen at the most exclusive hotels.'

'So I'm expensive?'

'At least a thousand pounds a night.'

'Not bad. I might try it.'

He laughed.

'What did he offer?'

'He didn't get round to a figure. I told him he couldn't afford me.'

'He can't.'

The two young men were still at the bar when Gina and Hugo went into dinner. She smiled at them.

Afterwards, they returned to the same alcove. There were few other people in the bar. She was beginning to feel pleasantly tipsy. They had maintained their pretence of prostitution.

'Of course, if you want anything different, it will be extra,' she said.

'Different? Such as what?'

'Bondage, for instance. I charge extra for being tied up.' His eyes widened and she knew she had hit the mark again. 'And I don't mind a little spanking, but it all costs that bit more.'

'I think I can afford it.'

The two young men returned to the bar with a third and older man. They sat on stools but kept glancing across the room.

'My admirer is back.'

Hugo looked towards them.

'Shall we go?'

'No. Let them look.' She licked her lips. 'Let them imagine.' She smiled. 'Why don't you go to the loo or something? Give them the chance to make another approach.'

'All right.'

He glanced around the room as he got up. The plant shielded them from other patrons. The only people who could see them were the three men at the bar. He leaned towards her and kissed her on the lips. As he did so, his hand rested on her knee and slid beneath the skirt.

When they broke apart she smiled into his face.

'You may have just devalued me.'

'Impossible.'

Hugo went to the men's room. The older man at the bar followed him. The two younger men walked towards her but sat at a table a short distance away. They sat facing her.

Gina felt the tension. It was in herself and in the situation. She had created a fantasy that three strange men believed. They thought she was a high-class prostitute. In their imagination they had already bought her and used her. They had imagined other men using her. Fucking her. She licked her lips and wondered if their pricks were hard. She crossed her legs and their eyes dipped like vultures.

Her husband came back. He looked bemused. A moment later, the third man joined the two others. She stared at Hugo.

'Well?'

'He asked me if you were my wife.'

'And?'

'I said no.'

'Go on.'

He pursed his lips.

'He was very diplomatic. He said you were beautiful. A stunner, was one of the terms he used. He asked if I'd known you long. I said I'd only met you tonight.'

Gina sipped the gin and tonic. Her insides were on meltdown. She loved the feeling of danger, of depravity so close and yet so safely on the other side of the dividing line of social convention.

'Get to the point.'

There had to be one.

'He asked how we had met. Between men of the world, he said. I said, between men of the world, that you were a company perk. That I was here on business and you had been provided for my pleasure.'

Gina kept expression from her face. She watched the three men at the other table talking together and looking at her.

'He said I was lucky. That the company must think a lot about me. He asked how much you cost. I said a thousand pounds.'

She ran her tongue along the underside of her top lip.

'Did he think the price too high?' she said.

'He said for that amount of money, you must be good. I said I'd been told you were exceptional.'

A waiter cleaned glasses at the bar. She wondered how they didn't break with the tension that now filled the bar. For a second, she had the urge to get up and leave, to go up to their room, lock the door and fuck her husband. But the second passed. The danger was still there, still waiting for a flirtation.

'Did he say anything else?' she said.

'He asked if you'd already been paid. I said you had. He asked if he could buy you afterwards.'

'What did you say?'

Hugo licked his lips.

'I said I'd ask.'

'Just him?'

'No. The three of them.'

'Afterwards?' she said, her voice almost breaking. 'Or before? Or all of you together?'

'Gina. We can go straight upstairs now.'

He had misunderstood the break in her voice. It had not

been caused because of outrage that he had listened to and relayed such a message. Or because he had presented the proposition as something she might consider. It was because the desire and fear had dried her throat.

A pulse moved in her neck with such strength she felt sure it was noticeable. It matched the feelings in her vagina and the pit of her stomach. Urgent, desperate feelings. This was not normal. Did Hugo know? Did he realise they were on the brink of the next dimension of their game?

'Are you turned on, Hugo?'

Her voice was normal. Almost eager.

'Yes.'

'So am I.'

She looked at the three men. Two young, one older. The blond and a young man with dark hair and a moustache. Regular features, good build.

The older man could be the father of the one who had spoken to her. He was a few inches shorter but broader. Short hair and bull neck. Close to fifty and wearing an expensive suit.

A provincial self-made man? A rough diamond with a thousand pounds to spend on a woman. A man who would be able to tell the tale at his golf club to impress his chums, as he would impress his son and his friend.

'What do you think, Hugo?'

'I don't know.'

He sounded desperate. He sounded as if he wanted someone to tell him what to think.

'Three strangers in a strange town. They've already undressed me in their minds. They've already fucked me. In their fantasy they've already had me. They'll have me again later when they fuck their girlfriends or their wives or masturbate. They'll think of me.'

The sex was building unbearably within her. She wasn't sure whether the words were thoughts or if she had been saying them out loud.

'Are you going to let them, Hugo?'

Her husband didn't speak.

She said, 'Have you imagined it? Three men having me at the same time? Have you, Hugo?'

'Yes,' he whispered.

'You could watch, Hugo. You could join in. You could wait in our room and I could tell you about it later.' She finished the drink but her mouth was still dry. 'It would just be a fantasy.'

The three men at the other table were watching them. She stared at the older man and nodded to him. He got up and came to the alcove and offered his hand. She gripped it briefly and he sat in a chair on the other side of the table.

'My name is Alec Smith.'

She smiled and he chuckled at her scepticism.

'It really is,' he said.

'Names are not important.'

Anonymity was important. Three strangers in a strange town.

Gina said, 'My client has told me of your offer.'

'I hope you're not offended.'

His voice was cultured. Had she made an incorrect assumption about him because of his build? Appearances could be deceptive. After all, he believed her to be a prostitute.

'Of course not,' she said.

'Have you considered the offer?'

'Can you afford me?'

'You can have cash. Unless you take American express?'

He smiled at her and glanced at Hugo to include him in the joke. He was self-confident and not embarrassed.

'Do you have a room here?' she said.

'Of course.'

'If we come to an arrangement, I will not require any money from you. I've already been paid. It depends upon the wishes of my client.' Gina was keeping her voice neutral, professional. Is this how professionals negotiated? Probably not. They would probably take the extra cash that was being offered. She inclined her head towards Hugo. 'Tonight I belong to this gentleman. It depends on whether or not he wants to watch you fuck me.'

Alec Smith licked his lips. He had not expected her to be so forthright and that magic word had removed the pretensions from their conversation. She felt that if they touched, electricity would spark. He looked at Hugo.

'What do you say?' He licked his lips again. His mouth had become a desert. 'I'm quite willing to pay the money to you.'

Hugo shook his head.

'This isn't about money.'

The man looked back at Gina. He smiled at her reassuringly but she could sense his desire.

'You're very beautiful,' he said. He kept looking at Gina although he now addressed his words to Hugo. 'Would you like to watch us fuck the young lady?' She knew he used the word to pay her back for taking him by surprise with her language. 'We won't take long.' His smile broadened. 'It would be a night to remember.'

A farewell orgy on the Titanic. The memory was a dim

warning in the back of her brain but she told it to go away.

Gina said, 'Would you allow us a moment to discuss it?'

Smith looked as if he was about to say something else, but shrugged and stood up. When she had first seen him, she had thought of his body as a threat, but now she admired its power. He moved back to the other table. Hugo was still hesitant. He needed resolve. He needed the onus of decision.

She said, 'If you say yes there are conditions.' He looked at her, sensing a lifeline. 'We go to their room but you're in charge. As soon as you say enough, it stops and we leave. You tell them that, Hugo. You have to be in charge.'

He nodded and she knew he was committed. She wondered if she would be able to walk to the lift. Her thighs were weak with want.

'You'd better tell them the conditions, Hugo. You'd better tell them your decision.'

Hugo got up and went to the other table. He leaned over it to talk to them. She picked up his brandy and drained it. The three seated men got to their feet. All four were now standing, staring at her, waiting. The blond-haired young man kept flicking his right hand in a nervous gesture. Her husband bit his bottom lip to stop it from trembling. He dared not meet her eyes.

Gina got to her feet and steadied herself with an outstretched hand on the back of the seat. It was another performance, that was all. Only the cast was bigger. She didn't have to learn any lines, she didn't even have to act. All she had to do was allow them to fuck her.

All decisions were now out of her control. She was

without guilt. Released from responsibility. She could be forced to perform sex, she could be forced to do the unthinkable. Forced to do what she wanted to do.

The group of men parted as she reached them and fell in, two on either side, like a guard of honour as they walked towards the lifts.

Chapter 28

Gina looked across the foyer at reception. A young couple waited for their key while the girl behind the desk spoke on the telephone. A man in uniform stood inside the front glass doors of the hotel. She could still walk away. Leave them, abandon the game.

The lift doors opened and she stepped inside and left normality behind. The four men followed her. The younger men stood behind her, the older in front. They all faced her and filled the small compartment. Alec Smith pressed for the fifth floor and the doors closed.

Before they had completely shut, hands touched her buttocks.

'Jesus,' whispered the blond boy.

He seemed to be having trouble with his breathing. The lift began to move slowly but he couldn't wait. He pulled the dress up, tugging at the material with shaking hands. She tensed and stared into the face of Smith who was watching her reaction. She did not react.

The dress was around her waist. Hands were on her flesh, above the stockings, feeling the softness of her buttocks, stroking the curves of her thighs. Someone was pushing against her hip. She could feel an erect penis beneath the cloth of his trousers.

Hugo stared at her. His eyes bulged. Hers widened as fingers went beneath her panties and rubbed against her vagina. They scratched in the pubic hair and found the lips of her sex. Fingers entered her.

'She's wet,' whispered the blond.

There was no space to move or protest, even if she had wanted to. She was trapped and helpless. Gloriously helpless. She moved her hand and touched the front of Hugo's trousers. His penis was huge.

The light showed the fifth floor and a bell pinged. The hands were removed and the dress pushed down. The doors opened and they stepped out, the men still close to her as if they feared she might run away. The corridor was quiet and empty.

Smith went ahead, a key in his hand. Hugo followed, glancing back at Gina. The two young men resumed touching her as they walked along the carpeted corridor. A hand beneath her dress, another on her breasts.

They reached the room and Smith opened the door. He went inside, switching on lights. Gina and the young men followed. Hugo was last.

Now that they were in an enclosed room and there was no escape, the hands left her. Gina dropped her bag on a chair and waited. The room contained two double beds. Hugo stood near the entrance, by the bathroom, his hands folded across his front like an undertaker. Waiting to take home the body?

Smith said, 'I apologise for the impatience of youth. I hope you will forgive them.'

Gina shrugged.

'Their impatience is a compliment.'

He opened the refrigerated bar and poured himself a neat whisky.

'Would you like anything?' he asked.

All she wanted was sex.

She shook her head. The men all stared at her. No, not at her, they stared at her body. Their eyes devoured her body. It was there to be taken, to be uncovered, and yet they waited, and their fervid imaginations continued to work.

The blond had highly flushed cheeks. His friend was breathing through his mouth and kept glancing at Hugo and Smith for reassurance.

Gina reached behind her and unzipped the dress. She shrugged it from her shoulders, held it a moment at her breasts, then allowed it to slide down. She held it and bent forward to step out of it. She threw it to Hugo.

'Well?' she said. 'Who's first?'

The two young men came at her simultaneously, eager to respond to her challenge. The blond took her in his arms and held her head and kissed her. She had not expected to be kissed. His lips pushed hers apart and his tongue dug into her mouth. Momentarily, she struggled but his grip was firm and she could not stop him.

Behind her, the dark-haired young man pulled at her panties. He pushed them from her buttocks until they hung around her thighs. His hands caressed the flesh and went between her legs. His fingers pushed and probed and parted the lips of her vagina. Gina gasped into the mouth that was kissing her as fingers dug into her.

The attack continued but the sequences were rushed. Youth was too impatient. They wanted everything at once and could not wait to indulge themselves. She was pushed to one of the beds. Her bra had been pulled partially down and her breasts hung from the cups. She was rolled onto her back on the mattress.

The blond boy knelt over her, his hands shaking as he fumbled with his trousers. Other hands pulled her panties from her legs. Her vision was partial, her mind as fragmented as their actions. Her legs were being spread and fingers were again inside her and she yelled at the suddenness of their insertion. The blond freed his penis and pushed it into her face. All she could see was his engorged manhood; his suit jacket shrouded the rest of the room from view.

'Suck it!' he begged.

She opened her mouth and sucked.

Between her legs, the fingers were removed. Someone knelt there, manoeuvred, and pushed a penis into her. The fucking began.

Gina closed her eyes and sucked. She held the shaft and used her mouth as enthusiastically as she could. She wanted to match the abandon of these eager young men. She wanted to lose her identity and become a willing recipient.

The blond was losing control. He pulled her hands away and pushed her arms above her head. He held her head and fucked her face.

Her arms were spread. She made no attempt to stop him, to stop either of them. She was the ultimate victim in the ultimate fantasy. She was not just flirting with danger, she was sucking it and being abused by it. This was not how it had happened in her imagination.

The man between her legs came but she was hardly aware of it for the penis in her mouth dominated her thoughts. Hands touched her. Her body was probed, but the touches were all ancillary to the hardness in her mouth. Finally, it disgorged and she choked as she swallowed the sperm that flooded her throat.

She gulped for air as the blond left her, and she could see once more. Alec Smith was between her legs and having sex with her but she had not been aware of it. He smiled into her face before lowering his head. He sucked her breasts. He caressed her buttocks.

He withdrew and she saw Hugo, still standing in the same position, still holding her dress, still watching. Like a pillar of salt.

Fire and brimstone.

Smith rolled her over, spread her legs, and entered her from behind. She groaned. This was her fire and brimstone. Was she damned?

Her emotions were new and old at the same time. This was so different to anything she had previously experienced. But she could not analyse it, not now. All she could do was suffer it.

Smith withdrew again and rolled her onto her side. He moved up the bed until his groin was by her face. He said nothing but offered his prick to her. It emerged from his fist, large and threatening, shiny with juices. She took hold of it, opened her mouth and sucked.

Behind her, she was being touched, groped. A penis was pushed between her thighs, her legs were spread and hands felt for the opening of her vagina. She was entered again. Whoever it was continued to be impatient. His abdomen slapped against her buttocks.

Her eyes were closed. This was fantasy, she told herself. In the morning she would awake and tell Hugo of her dream. Tell him a story.

More hands touched her. Pulled at her breasts. Pinched

her nipples and sent sharp pains coursing through her body. All the pains, all the sensations, all the currents went the same way. They went to her vagina. They bypassed her little beast, for he had become redundant, and filled her vagina. Her mind had become blank, her emotions shipwrecked. Only the physical remained.

The men moved. The bodies changed places. Words were exchanged and she was pulled down the bed and over its edge. She knelt on the carpet. The dark-haired young man was on the bed. He wore a jacket, shirt and tie, shoes and socks, but no trousers. The image was surreal. Was she part of a painting?

She was pushed forward and leaned onto the bed and took his penis in her mouth and sucked. That was what her mouth was for, wasn't it? To suck. Another penis entered her from behind and gained greater depth of entry. Her mind drifted again. There was no point in thought. She reacted to their limb-shaking urgency. She was sex.

Gina devoured the penis in her mouth with a sudden new enthusiasm that pushed it into her throat and made its owner come. The man shook and made strange noises. She didn't attempt to swallow but, when he moved away, allowed his discharge to seep from her lips onto the bed.

Her arms were spread above her once more. A fallen angel, always a victim. Words were exchanged behind her and the penis was withdrawn from her vagina. She didn't understand what was happening but felt a new surge of danger. Someone was arguing. She vaguely recognised the voice. Hugo? Was Hugo here?

Smith's voice was dominant. It silenced argument. It silenced the room except for the grunts of exertion of the man behind her. Fingers spread the slickness between her legs and over her buttocks. She moaned and knew what was about to happen. It was inevitable. Complete domination demanded it. She put her face into the mattress and bit into the bed covers as he forced an entry into her final orifice.

The intrusion suffused her with heat and pain. Her body was a sacrifice. It was torn and anguished and on fire. The pounding was the only rhythm she had ever known. It was all-consuming. It swept her away and she lost consciousness.

Gina became aware of someone staring into her face. Her body was numb. Empty. She opened her eyes. At the back of her mind, she expected to see her husband. Instead, she saw Alec Smith. He held her head and stroked the damp hair from her sweat-stained face. Something dribbled from her mouth and she licked her lips. The liquid was glutinous and salty. She remembered.

Other men were in the room behind Smith but she couldn't identify them. She couldn't work out very much at all except she had been crucified over the end of a bed. The room was hot. It smelled of sex. Smith was speaking to her, quietly, one to one, but first, she had to recover her mind to understand what he said.

'You're no whore,' he whispered. 'I know.' He smiled, a sympathetic smile. An understanding smile. 'You do it because you like it. Don't you?'

She closed her eyes and sensed him move behind her. He knelt between her legs, stroking her thighs, running his palms from the sheen of the stockings across her flesh. His penis lay in the groove of her buttocks. He moved the head slowly in the wetness. The valley had become flooded.

Her hips moved. Her buttocks contracted, tempting him. He raised himself and pushed the glans into the tightest sleeve. She groaned. No pretence, no hiding. She opened herself and pushed against him as he pushed, and it slid inside.

He had exchanged words with her but he had called no truce. He was giving nothing, simply taking. He sodomised her and she lay beneath him until he reached his climax. This time she retained consciousness. This time she sensed the cycle was complete.

The man moved away from her. She heard the noise of the mattress on the other bed as he collapsed upon it. One of the younger men laughed self-consciously. The blond boy.

Gina dragged her senses back. It was as if she gripped the strands in her hand like the strings of a parachute and drew them in until the canopy enclosed her. Someone was by her side, touching her arm, wanting to help. She needed no help.

She pushed Hugo's hand away and got to her feet. The scenario had not taken long to play out. Amazingly, her composure returned. Her jaw ached and her mouth felt bruised. The feeling between her legs was different. It made her tired. She took deep breaths. This had not been a marathon but a sprint relay.

Hugo held the dress but did not offer it. He did not seem to know how to behave or how she would behave. She took the dress from him, held it open and stepped into it. He held her arms as she almost lost her balance, but she stepped away from him and pulled the dress up, fitting her breasts into her bra and the bodice at the same time.

She stepped in front of him and stared at the two young men ambivalently. It had been an unforgettable experience and they were not sure what their roles had been. The blond boy blushed.

'Zip me up,' she said to her husband.

He did so.

Her panties were on the floor. She pointed and Hugo picked them up. Alec Smith still lay on the other bed, his clothes dishevelled. He smiled and nodded to her. His look said: I know.

'Magnificent,' he said.

Gina walked slowly across the room. She could not walk any other way. She paused by the two young men and looked at the blond. His blush deepened.

'Thank you,' he said, lamely.

She smiled.

'You still can't afford me,' she said softly.

'I know.'

Did he know, like his father knew? Had he realised she was not for sale at any price? That Hugo was her husband?

Gina touched his cheek briefly in farewell and left the room without looking back. Her husband followed behind her.

She reached the lift unaided but once inside she leaned against him for support. He held her as they went down to the second floor. His body trembled and his hands were unsure.

'I tried to stop them,' he said.

'It doesn't matter,' she said. 'It didn't happen.'

They went along another corridor and he opened the door to their room. They went inside and the door closed. She held him.

'Don't put on the light,' she said.

She reached behind her and unzipped the dress. She shrugged it from her shoulders and stepped away from his body so that it fell around her feet. She leaned against him again. His erection was huge in his trousers.

Gina took his hand and put it between her legs. She directed his fingers into the wetness, into her vagina that gaped like a wound.

'They were useless, Hugo,' she whispered. 'I need you.'

Chapter 29

Gina was at the restaurant first. She sipped a glass of red wine. Perhaps Mario had sensed a change in her. For the first time he had attempted to flirt as he recommended the pasta with truffles.

Hugo had also sensed a change in her. They had left the hotel in Leeds early the next morning to avoid any embarrassing encounters over breakfast and had driven to Newcastle. His attendance at the conference was only required for one day but that proved too much and he cancelled.

Instead, they stayed in their hotel room and had sex all day. They drove back through the night. He had become over-protective towards her and desired her more than ever. For the first time, they had sex in his office. But they still had not spoken of what happened. Perhaps he would speak of it, when time had healed his conscience. In the dark of the night in the bedroom when he felt able, once again, to request a story.

Gina knew he would. Eventually. She had learned a lot about her husband and men in the last few weeks. A lot about herself, too. She had never before fully appreciated her own capacity for life.

Sam arrived and grinned as Mario led her across the restaurant. They kissed.

'You look pleased with yourself,' Gina said.

'I'm going to Singapore.'

'Gin slings and Raffles?'

'And Brian.'

'That's great.'

Gina poured wine into Sam's glass. Sam took a good drink.

'It's been a hectic morning,' she said. 'By the way, Carol Purley may have some work for you. If you're still interested.'

'I'm interested. I've made a few calls myself. I've got an offer from my old firm. A couple of days a week to start but Charlie sounded keen to have me back.'

'Good for you.'

Mario came and took their orders. Gina acquiesced and had the pasta with truffles.

Sam said, 'How was Somerset?'

'Would you like to read about it?'

'Will it put me off my food?'

'I would think so.'

'Then let's eat first.'

After the meal, Sam read the photocopied pages of the journal that related to the weekend in the country with Philip. When she had finished, she looked at her friend.

'So you've gone the whole way?'

'Yes.'

'Hugo was impressed. How was it for you?'

They smiled at the archness of the question.

'Rather bloody marvellous, actually.'

'Really?'

Sam licked her lips.

Gina wondered if Sam might consider something similar in the future. When she had got over the novelty of her husband's infatuation.

'Really,' Gina said.

'Will you do it again?'

'I don't know.' During photocopying, Gina had deleted the reference to repeating the experiment when circumstances permitted. 'I don't think Hugo wants to.'

She handed Sam another photocopied page.

'What's this?'

'The last entry.'

Across it was written: No more.

Sam said, 'So the journal is complete? He did know when to stop?'

'Yes.' Gina smiled. 'He did.'

'Any regrets?'

'None.'

How could she have any regrets when her life had opened so dramatically? When her orgasm in a hotel room had been so immense it had caused her to pass out? How could she tell even Sam about it?

Sam had moved on and so had she.

The bull-necked man had seen through the game and so, she suspected, had Hugo. She liked it. She liked everything about it. Lust AND romance.

What was more, Hugo knew he had lost control. He knew he no longer possessed her in the same way, that he could no longer direct her through the pages of a journal with a discreet dialogue. He knew that now she belonged to no-one but herself.

'What about the book?' Sam said, jokingly.

Gina said, 'I still think it's a valid proposition.' She sipped red wine. 'But it needs more research.' She smiled over the rim of the glass. 'I've started my own journal. Are you interested?'